The Alpenhaus

WHERE LOST DREAMS AWAKEN - BOOK ONE

CHERILYN CHRISTEN CLOUGH

LITTLE RED PRESS

To Jeannie Robinson,
a dear friend.
Although we've never met in person,
your ideas as you've edited my books
have given me wonderful ways
to improve my stories.
Thank you.

Contents

I saw your smile
I felt your warmth
I sensed your spirit
Before I ever felt your touch.

Even then I knew
The scent of your hair,
The sound of your voice
Echoing off these hills
Would never be too much.

Prologue

GLARUS, SWITZERLAND, AUGUST 22, 1843

Amalia took a deep breath and glanced up at the Romanesque church tower pointing toward the azure sky. Built five hundred years earlier, it was the tallest building in the village. Inside, she could hear the organ playing her favorite hymn, "*Now Thank We All Our God.*" She nervously touched the wreath of wildflowers resting atop her exquisitely braided brown hair—just a quick check to make sure it was still in place. Then, holding a bouquet of yellow violets in one hand, she reached for her father's arm with the other and took the step that would change her life forever.

It was the wedding she'd always dreamed about—flowers, food, music. Everything was perfect, except for one thing—she was marrying the wrong man.

This wasn't her original plan, but she wanted more than anything to be good, and good daughters were expected to obey their fathers. Despite her lack of affection, Herr Grob had assured his daughter that she would learn to love her new husband.

Along with submitting to her father, she was getting something in return—a good provider who would ensure a stable home to raise her children.

It was a small wedding, and the guests didn't begin to fill the austere church, but Amalia's family and friends came to wish her well. Many of the guests, along with her parents, believed she was making a good match because the groom was a carpenter and shouldn't lack for work.

In the Canton of Glarus, Switzerland, in 1843, the small farming community of Obstalden was struggling. Famines, sickness, and weather patterns had destroyed crops and disrupted life for over a decade. Despite hard times, the community came out to celebrate the union, bringing their best cheese, wine, and potato dishes.

While the minister rambled on about the duties of marriage, Amalia's eyes wandered to the washed-out mural on the tower's wall. Painted by the church fathers three centuries earlier, it was a fading reminder that human lives are short while God alone is eternal.

She lowered her eyes in shame as she imagined a cloud of holy witnesses watching her make this solemn promise—to marry one man—while she loved another.

In those moments before she said, "I do," she pondered which was the greater sin—to disobey her father or marry a man she didn't love. Did she even have a choice?

As soon as the preacher declared them man and wife, the new couple stepped outside to light the bride's wreath. The groom lifted the wildflowers from Amalia's head and handed the symbol of her virginity to his bride. Swiss tradition predicted that the faster the wreath burned, the better the bride's luck. They smiled at each other while the groom's cousin Anton held up the torch.

Afterward, rumors spread that Anton had been distracted by an eagle flying overhead and took too long to light the wreath, while others wondered if it had ever been adequately lit. Regardless, a strong wind came up from behind and snuffed out the flame.

Women gasped, men groaned, and gossips turned to each other, asking what it meant.

Unflustered, Amalia looked up at the sky. She figured it was a reminder that God was sovereign. If she were going to have good luck, it would depend on divine timing, and she must remain patient.

The shocked villagers remained silent, staring at the unlit wreath, until someone shouted, "Throw the bouquet!"

Ever compliant, Amalia turned her back to the crowd. She imagined that some young girl would catch it and put it under her pillow to dream about her future husband, as she had once done.

Tossing the flowers over her shoulder, she caught sight of the turquoise lake far below the village and winced as a pang of regret hit her stomach.

She ached, not only for what was—but for what might have been.

1 Walensee

Amalia was thirteen when her parents took her to a wedding down by the Walensee. At the time, she had no dreams of marrying anyone. She felt awkward—too old to sit with the children, yet too young to be considered an adult. Wandering among the wedding guests, seeking a place to belong, she noticed a tall teenager standing at the back of the crowd.

Her schoolmate Ursula noticed her staring and came over to whisper, "That's Peter Britt, brother of the groom."

The guests had just finished toasting the bride and groom when Peter and several other young men stepped forward to sing a song for the newlyweds. Amalia's heart thrilled to hear their harmony, but it was the young man in the middle who kept her attention. He turned his eyes away when she looked at him, but his confidence, mixed with an awkward vulnerability, intrigued her.

She couldn't imagine an older boy like him finding her attractive—she barely had breasts, and wore her hair in two childlike braids hanging down to her waist. Her self-consciousness kept her from noticing that Peter was trying to grow a thin mustache in the hope of looking like a man.

When the guests tapped spoons on the wine glasses for the newlyweds to kiss, Amalia looked at Peter. She wondered how he would respond to his brother kissing the bride. Then she laughed, when he wrinkled his nose like something in the room smelled rotten. Before she knew it, Peter was beside her, making jokes as if a wedding was not a solemn occasion.

The newly married couple danced in the golden light as the sun fell toward the horizon. The village folk flitted around them in laughter and song—until suddenly, there was a skirmish, and somebody kidnapped the bride.

While the groom and his friends ran off to find her, an older man turned to Peter. "Aren't you going to help your brother find his wife?"

Peter acted as if he hadn't heard the man and turned to Amalia. "Would you like to go down to the lake?"

Amalia glanced toward her father before she agreed. She hoped he wouldn't notice her walking toward the lake with a boy.

Across the lake, the nearly vertical cliffs of the mountains formed a formidable rock wall. The Walensee always wore turquoise in the sunshine—and this day was no exception. As one of the largest lakes in Switzerland, it carried the waters from three glacial rivers and deposited them into the Linth Canal. Boats from Obstalden traveled down the lake, into the Linth, and onto the larger world.

As they followed the short trail to the lake, the brisk March wind warned them that it was far too cold for swimming. Peter stopped to pick up a handful of rocks before they sat on the dock.

The teenagers skipped rocks across the water while each tried to think of something to say.

"I've never thought a wedding could be so much fun." Peter's voice was soft and husky.

Amalia giggled. "This is the most interesting thing I've done all year."

She wasn't talking about the wedding. She meant talking to a boy beside the lake. And she hoped she didn't sound as nervous as she felt.

"Well, if this is the most interesting thing you'll do all year, I feel sorry for you. I'm planning to travel through France and Germany this summer."

Amalia bit her lip before answering. "The thought of getting on a boat and traveling down the Linth sounds frightening."

Peter slid closer to her. "You just need the right traveling companion."

She hoped he wouldn't notice her cheeks growing warm.

The winter sun slid below the horizon, while the sounds of singing and laughter echoed across the lake as the party continued above them. That night there was no moon. As the shadows gathered around them, they could barely make out the Alps that guarded their simple and ancient way of life. The sky was cloudless, and the stars soon popped into view, one by one.

Peter motioned toward a falling star. "Ptolemy said the stars are a sure sign that God is listening to our wishes. Would you like to make one?"

Amalia smiled. "Can we both make a wish? Or is there only one wish per star?"

Peter laughed, "I don't know, but the one thing you can't do is tell me what you wish for."

Amalia tossed the last rock from her hand into the water. "I wouldn't do that—or it might never come true."

"Smart girl!" Peter handed her a rock from his hand. He placed it in her palm, and gently wrapped her fingers around it one by one, as if experimenting to see how much she'd allow him to touch her. When he stretched out on his back to gaze at the stars, Amalia followed his example. They lay on the dock, comparing childhood stories about snow forts and ruined Christmas surprises from peeking behind their parents' backs.

"Have you ever been to Quinten? It's just across the lake, where they have more sun than we have here in Glarus. They can even grow grapes over there."

"No, I've never even left the Canton."

A large boat passed with lanterns swinging from both sides, and the dock began to rock in its wake. Peter reached out to hold her hand as if to steady her.

Amalia looked from the water to the sky. "I heard that a fisherman could get lost between the stars on the water and the stars in the sky, on a dark, moonless night like this." Her voice trailed off almost to a whisper. "And possibly drown."

Peter chuckled. "I doubt that would happen if they just stayed on the boat."

His common sense made her laugh too. Something about this boy filled her with a sense of calm.

As his face grew closer to hers, Amalia held her breath. Her face had never been so close to a boy before. She was shutting her eyes, hoping he might kiss her, when the door to the house above them opened.

Her father's gruff voice broke into her thoughts. "Amalia! Where are you? Let's go!"

Peter dropped her hand and vanished, leaving Amalia alone on the dock. Puzzled by his abrupt departure, her eyes searched the shoreline and peered into the starry depths, but the water and the trees remained still.

For a moment, she wondered if she'd imagined this encounter. Her eyes searched for a sign that this wasn't a dream. Hadn't they breathed the same air and stared at the same stars? Hadn't he touched her hand and leaned in close enough that she could smell the farm on him? Or had she just imagined it? Then her fingers felt the smooth rock in her hand, and she knew it was true.

Herr Grob impatiently called out again. "Amalia, where are you? I sure hope you're not alone with that boy."

Amalia stood up and steadied herself against the pier before answering. "Of course not. Coming, *Vater*!"

2 Wind

As soon as Amalia entered the schoolhouse, her eyes searched for Peter's tall, lanky frame. Before the wedding, he'd been just another boy, but his mysterious charm had awakened her curiosity, and now she couldn't forget the sound of his laughter echoing off the lake.

Even though she'd spent the evening with him, she knew so little about him. She wished she'd asked him more questions. Did he enjoy singing, or had his family forced him to perform for his brother's wedding? She wondered what he liked to do besides travel—or how he even found the means. He didn't appear wealthy, and his clothing was simple like the rest of the farmers in Obstalden.

In the month since the wedding, Amalia had wondered many things, but they were all swallowed up by one question—where was Peter Britt? Why hadn't he been to school? Had he already left for his travels? Perhaps he had stopped going to school months ago to work on the farm. She marveled that a boy she hadn't noticed for years had become the most exciting person in the village overnight.

When the last group of boys filed into the building with no sign of Peter, Amalia slid into her desk at the back of the room and listened carefully as the roll was called. She was relieved to hear his name—even though he was nowhere in sight. It gave her hope to think he might be back someday.

This time, as his name was called, someone raised their hand. It was a younger boy she'd seen at the wedding. "That's my cousin, sir! He's helping our Onkel with the cows."

So that was it? Amalia sighed with relief as she looked out the window, longing for a glimpse of Peter.

The teacher called the class to order and wrote an arithmetic problem on the chalkboard. Amalia had just begun the long division on her slate when a strong gust of wind blew the door shut with a bang. She braced herself as a flash of light swept through her vision.

It wasn't the slamming of the door, but the dreaded wind that bothered her. There was nothing like a hot wind to set people's nerves on edge. Many Glarner people got headaches when the winds came. A few even went crazy. No one knew for sure if the winds themselves caused these maladies, or if it was the fear of what the winds were capable of doing. Hot foehn winds had been known to destroy crops, steal the snow from the mountains, and start fires with little notice. Houses burned, crops failed, and people went hungry—all because of these quick-moving hot winds.

Some said the foehn winds came straight from hell, but her father often said, "The Lord giveth and the Lord taketh away." Amalia always shuddered when he said this. She wasn't sure she liked that side of God.

As a pine branch blew past the window, Amalia placed a hand on her left temple to check the sensation in her head. Then, she raised her hand to get the teacher's attention.

"I need to go home; I feel a headache coming on."

The schoolmaster, familiar with her headaches, waved permission for her to leave—the sooner, the better. And hopefully, before she threw up on his shoes—as she had done when she was younger.

Ursula Brunner watched anxiously out the window as Amalia walked away from the schoolhouse. She longed to be with Amalia whenever the foehn winds came, but the teacher called the class back to order and told her to solve the first problem on the board.

When Amalia stepped outside, she could barely see the path before her due to the bright sunlight. As often happened during one of her headaches, even the most beautiful things brought pain. Light reflections off the lake bore into her vision as if an ice pick were chopping at her left eye. As she passed a farm boy leading his cow home, she winced with every clang of its bell. It felt like someone was pounding inside her head. The left side of her face was beginning to go numb. It was all she could do to focus on one step at a time.

Trudging up the hill, she struggled to keep her eyes open. She was desperate to get home, where she could shut the curtains and go to bed. Thus, she marched on with little notice of anything around her. Amid the flashing lights and auras, she imagined she saw Peter Britt. When the smell of manure made her stomach lurch, she rushed as far away from the stench as possible—until she heard someone calling her name.

"Amalia?"

Was that his voice? She must be imagining things. When he spoke again, she realized it was Peter standing in front of her. He was hauling a wagonload of manure drawn by a mule.

"How are you, Amalia?"

"I'm good." It was a lie, but Amalia was trying to keep her composure. She tried to make her voice sound cheerful and friendly, but she wasn't at her best.

When she stumbled over a rock in the road, Peter's expression changed to concern when he realized she wasn't well. "Are you feeling poorly?"

Amalia struggled to smile through the pain. "I'll be okay. I get these headaches, but they go away once the winds are gone."

"Here, allow me to give you a ride home." He motioned to the seat beside him on the wagon.

She shook her head as the bile rose to her throat. The last person she wanted to be sick in front of was Peter Britt.

"I'll be okay." It wasn't true, but she hated how vulnerable she felt—especially in front of him.

As she passed by, Peter called over his shoulder, "My mutter makes tea to help with that. I'll ask her to bring you some."

"Danke." Amalia stumbled again as she rushed up the steps to her home. Her heart sank to think how she'd been so eager to see Peter just an hour before, and now it seemed she'd made a fool of herself. She tried to analyze their conversation, but the pain demanded her full attention.

Once she was home, Maria Grob rushed to help her daughter out of her school clothes and into bed. Then she hurried downstairs to get a cool, damp cloth for her daughter's forehead.

Amalia closed her eyes and tried to relax until she remembered what Peter said. She sat back up. "Peter's sending his mother to our house." She moaned. "Why now—while I'm in such a state? Oh, how embarrassing!"

Her mother insisted she lie back down, so Amalia shut her eyes again, wishing the headache, the winds, and that awkward encounter with Peter would all disappear.

Minutes later, she was vaguely aware of a knock at the door. As she kicked the warm duvet to the foot of the bed, she could hear her mother's muffled greeting.

A short time later, her mother tiptoed into her room with a cup of tea.

"I'd let it cool a little, but Frau Britt says it will calm your stomach."

Amalia sat up to take a sip.

"She's invited you to their Alpenhaus this summer, where you can gather herbs and learn to make your own tea."

Amalia set the mug down and leaned back onto the pillow, pulling the damp cloth back over her eyes.

"Do you think Vater would allow me to do that?"

"I can't imagine why not—we've known the Britts our entire lives. They're good people."

An hour later, Amalia handed the empty cup to her mother. "The sickness seems to be fading. Perhaps I can sleep now."

Maria Grob tucked the cool linen sheet across her daughter's shoulder. Calmed by visions of lush alpine meadows and wildflowers, Amalia drifted off as the image of Peter Britt's face blurred into her dreams.

3 Willow

WHEN AMALIA WOKE UP, it was dark. Reaching for a blanket to wrap around her shoulders, she stepped to the window and opened the sash. What a relief to feel the cool, fresh air—a sure sign that the hot foehn wind had passed. A breeze rose from the lake, stirring the willow in the front yard.

Even though she'd been sleeping for hours, she was up earlier than usual and the sky was still dark. She sat down at the writing desk her father had built for her, and waited for the morning light.

Her little room was pleasant throughout the seasons. In the winter, the chimney climbed through her room, adding warmth on its way to the attic. In summer, a cool breeze came up from the lake and carried the spicy scent of geraniums from the planter her father hung outside her window. On a chair beside her bed, sat a rag doll that Amalia had barely touched since she was eight.

Over her bed hung one of her proudest accomplishments—an embroidery sampler she'd finished when she was twelve. The needlework was sewn in green with the alphabet across the top and numbers on the bottom. In the middle, she'd painstakingly stitched a poem from a primer. She couldn't see it in the dim morning light, but she could recite it from memory.

> *Though none can doubt*
> *God's generous love,*
> *Immeasurable and kind,*
> *To His unerring gracious will*
> *Be every wish resigned.*
> *Good, when He gives,*
> *Supremely good,*
> *Not less when He denies,*
> *Even crosses from*
> *His sovereign hand*
> *Are blessings in disguise.*
> *—Anonymous*

Amalia had not yet reached the place where she could see the blessings in disguise, but the faith of her parents encouraged her to accept that God was sovereign and had a plan for her life.

The rooster crowing next door sounded louder than usual through the open window. She hoped he wouldn't wake her little brother Fridolin, or he might pound on her door to see if she was awake and ask for a story.

She knew it was only a matter of time before the church bells would peal. Amalia was used to the routine. Every morning, the neighbor across the street opened her window to toss out the contents of the water pot. Then the shopkeeper further down the hill would step outside to sweep his porch. Next, five-year-old Fridolin's voice would carry past her room as he called for their mother to help him get dressed.

Maria Grob was devoted to her family. It seemed to be her pleasure to care for them by cooking and making their home cozy. Their neighbors knew her as a kind woman, and she usually was—unless her family came late to breakfast.

Herr Grob was a carpenter by trade. He could build anything and was not only a good provider but also well respected in both the Village and the wider community. He always paid his bills and kept his family in line. He was a member in good standing at the Christian Reformed Church, where he and his family always arrived on time for Sunday services.

The Village community could never recall faulting Herr Grob for anything. To his neighbors, he was steady, dependable, and unfailingly proper. Yet behind closed doors, his temper ruled the household. He reserved his sharpest words and harshest moods for his wife and children, who had long since learned not to argue. When he was in an angry mood, they moved quietly through the house he had built for them, careful to stay out of his way and wait, in tense silence, for the storm to pass.

To be fair, Herr Grob was not a cruel man. He loved his wife and children, but he followed the tradition of many religious fathers who believed they must beat their children into submission to ensure they followed God's will. Amalia understood that her father would never tolerate the idea of her being in danger—or of taking advice from anyone but him. Yet as she grew older, she found it increasingly troubling that her father and God always seemed to share the same will. The rules often felt less like guidance and more like shackles.

From the time she was small, she knew where Herr Grob kept the willow switch on the back porch. It amazed her that the same tree she loved to sit beneath on warm summer days could deliver such a cruel sting when turned against her legs. If she dared to cross her father's will, punishment always followed. Over time, she decided it was safer to avoid both the beatings and the submission—often by lying.

If all her efforts failed and she felt the brunt of his anger, Amalia turned to her mother for comfort and refuge. One day, when she was six, she forgot to latch the door, and let all the chickens loose. Before she could catch them, a hawk swooped down and carried one off. Fearing the wrath of the willow switch, Amalia ran sobbing to her mother, who hid her in her parents' bedroom until the storm passed. Her father never thought to look there because he only entered that room to sleep.

Herr Grob also believed in hard work—even for children—and he did not approve of Amalia going to Ursula's house after school to play. In his view, it was far better for her to come straight home, assist her mother with supper, or practice useful skills like embroidery and sewing.

Though Amalia enjoyed these quiet pursuits and took pleasure in helping her mother, there was a special joy in visiting Ursula's home. Before Fridolin came along, Amalia had no other siblings. She and her cousin Barbara—also an only child—had formed a close-knit circle of friendship with Ursula, whose house stood conveniently near the school and rang with the cheerful clamor of brothers and sisters at play.

One afternoon, Herr Grob demanded to know why Amalia had arrived home so late. She had stopped by Ursula's house after school, but fearing the willow stick, she told him that the teacher had kept her behind to work on arithmetic. Herr Grob believed her, but Maria did not. Careful not to challenge Amalia in front of her husband, Maria waited until they were preparing supper to ask gently, "Why did you lie to your Vater?"

Amalia met her mother's gaze without flinching. "It never pays to tell Vater the truth," she said quietly. "He only gets angry."

Maria's only reply was a sympathetic nod. From that day on, Amalia began to lie to Herr Grob to sidestep his rigid rules—with her mother's unspoken consent. She reasoned that if she were ever caught, her father's forgiveness would come more easily than his permission. Yet she was seldom caught. Over time, Amalia became adept at hiding the truth, and Herr Grob rarely questioned her, or suspected otherwise.

Despite his temper and strictness, Amalia knew she still held a special place in her father's heart. Maria had lost several babies before Amalia came, and she had become her father's pet. He often indulged her with bedtime stories, pretty dress material at Christmas, and small treats her mother frowned upon. Herr Grob always bought the best for his girl—at least until his son came along.

A faint glow on the horizon revealed that it was almost morning. The Grob house stood at the upper end of the village, and in the deepening light, Amalia could see nearly everything that served their lives from her vantage point. As streaks of golden yellow and bright pink scattered across the dark purple sky, her eyes searched for the familiar landmarks.

There was the school where she tried to beat the boys in arithmetic. Ursula's house was just a few doors down from the school. Next came the village shops, which included a tavern, a blacksmith, a bakery, a butcher, and a general store that carried a little something for everyone.

The Obstalden Reformed Church overshadowed all other buildings in the landscape. Herr Grob declared it the most important landmark in their village. Its tower, pointing to the sky, constantly reminded the community that God was ever-present. The church also recorded births, marriages, and deaths. Some people would argue that the lake was just as important, because it watered their gardens and gave them a route for travel and trade. Together, the church and the lake had remained for centuries, while the people and their lives came and went.

Shutting the window, Amalia turned back and opened the armoire to find her petticoat. The scent of lavender filled her nose. Every year, for as long as she could remember, her mother made new sachets to fill the beds and dressers to ward off spiders and fleas.

Amalia always hesitated before she opened her bedroom door. She was in danger of being knocked over by five-year-old Fridolin, who often raced down the stairs as if he were skiing. Her little brother was always hungry and, in her opinion, quite spoiled. She tried not to let it bother her that both parents seemed to favor him. And why shouldn't they? He was their long-awaited male heir and still innocent enough to be cute. Even Amalia was not immune to his charms.

Standing at the foot of the stairs, Maria Grob called for her family to start their day. "Amalia! Fridolin! Time to break the fast!"

Amalia knew they would all make it downstairs on time for breakfast, where her father would read from the Bible before thanking God for the food.

As she finished braiding her hair, Amalia slid into her dress and tied her apron. By the time she laced her shoes, the Walensee had turned a glorious bright pink. This was her favorite time of day, and she paused for a moment to take in the view. Across the lake, where the Alps rose straight to the sky, the sun began to spill over their peaks. Amalia held her breath as she watched it bring light to the Village.

Her mother's delicious cooking, her father's deep voice reading the Bible, her brother's affectionate teasing, and this cozy attic room made up the rhythm of her days.

She knew no other home, but something inside her had changed since the wedding. She loved her family, but she had begun to dream of a home and family of her own. Before she turned to go downstairs, Amalia's eyes squinted at the horizon. She wondered if she could see the Britt place from her window.

4 Wildflowers

Amalia's lungs screamed for air as she followed Dorothea Britt up the mountain. She was used to walking uphill, but she'd never had a reason to climb so high. Despite being decades older, her companion seemed unaffected by the cold wind, thin air, and rocky cliffs.

When Dora, as her friends called her, stopped to pick some purple daisy-like flowers, Amalia collapsed onto a rock to catch her breath. She turned to look back at the trail behind them. It wound through green grass and rocky outcroppings like a tan ribbon, leading to the valley far below. In the distance, the Walensee shone like a giant emerald, while the Obstalden church had never looked so small.

A frigid wind tore down the mountain, bringing a scraggly grove of trees to life like a row of dancing puppets. Shivering, Amalia pulled her blue cap tighter around her ears. Cool breezes were expected at the high altitude, but they did nothing to stir her fears like the hot Foehn winds that had swept through the canton a few weeks earlier.

The Britt family owned a small farm in Obstalden, but they often made the trek to their ancestral cabin. It was a manageable hike when the weather cooperated. This year, the foehn winds had melted much of the snow early, leaving the trail bare. It had made their journey easier, but left many wondering whether the water supply would hold up throughout the summer.

That morning, Amalia had enjoyed gathering sap from the trees near the cabin, while Dora shared stories of the Britt ancestors—how they'd farmed the land and raised cattle for generations. As a bonus, Amalia had met Peter's *Onkel* Andreas, who lived there year-round and tended the cows during the summer months.

Dora explained how spring was the best time to harvest the sap while it was running. She used several types of sap in her potions. Spruce sap could be used as a wound salve. Pine resin could be mixed with lard as a warming balm for rheumatism. Scraping the sap had been messy, but it was the climb to the top of the mountain—searching among steep, rocky cliffs—that left Amalia exhausted.

Dora stepped over a patch of ice and melting snow to reach some tall plants with fern-like leaves. After slicing through the tough stems with a knife, she handed one to Amalia.

"Sheep's herb has many uses. We'll soak this in brandy to make a stomach-soothing potion. And these leaves, when applied directly to a wound, can stop bleeding. We can also make a tea made from the flowers, which will bloom later in the season. This plant can heal all kinds of ailments." Dora's eyes lit up with joy at the thought of what she could make to help others.

Amalia ran her finger over the leathery leaves, then crushed them between her fingers. A sharp, piney scent rose in the mountain air. She remembered her mother giving her an elixir when she was small, something warm and bitter when her stomach ached. Maybe it had come from this very herb.

Despite the sun, the air was cold. Amalia thought about jumping up and down to stay warm, if only she wasn't so exhausted from climbing. She was ready to return to the Alpenhaus, but to her dismay, Dora continued climbing. The young woman trailed behind, wondering how much longer she could keep up.

The whole point of coming up the mountain was to visit the Alpenhaus, and hopefully catch a glimpse of Peter. But now they had wandered far beyond the little cabin, into a wilderness where no humans were likely to appear—let alone the object of her affection.

At the top of a rise, Dora paused, and a gentle smile played on her lips while she gazed up at the cliffs above them.

"When I was a girl, I came up here with my grandmother," she said. "She told me stories about the days when these trails were full of wild mountain goats—creatures that could walk straight up the side of a cliff and warn of an avalanche before it came. It was considered good luck to see one. But so many were hunted that they've all but disappeared. I haven't seen one since I was a child, and even then, they were rare.

"Everything we do, whether we harvest pitch from the trees, or pluck flowers from the meadows, must be done respectfully because it will affect nature. When people take too much, it upsets the balance. And sometimes, nature doesn't spring back."

With a wistful sigh, Dora stepped carefully around another clump of melting snow.

"Ah, there they are!" She knelt to brush aside a layer of dead leaves, then motioned for Amalia to come closer.

A cluster of small yellow flowers peeked out from a tumble of rocks. They reminded Amalia of something between a dandelion and a daisy—but without any leaves.

Dora quickly snipped the blooms from their stems and tucked them into the leather rucksack slung over her shoulder.

"This is coltsfoot. It helps treat coughs and fevers—especially this time of year, when so many fall prey to such illnesses."

Known in the community for her green thumb, it was Dora's knack for using wild plants, alongside those from her garden, that made her concoctions so sought-after. Few people took the time or care to craft such unique potions.

"How do you know which plants to use?" Amalia was beginning to feel a little curious in spite of herself.

"Most of the recipes came from my Britt ancestors," Dora replied. "They were healers."

Amalia knew Peter's parents shared the same last name, but that didn't necessarily mean they were related. In Glarus, family names had been passed around for centuries. Her own surname, Grob, was just as common.

Dora gave her a warm smile. "I seem to be the last of the line. Maybe I can pass the potions on to you. I'd hate for them to be lost."

Amalia shifted her weight from one rock to another. She didn't want to disappoint her new friend—but truth be told, she was far more interested in Dora's son than in tinctures and teas.

"Gathering flowers to make tea is a lot more work than picking a few blossoms for my pressed flower collection," she spoke casually, hoping it would serve as a gentle hint.

Dora winked. "It gets easier once you know where to look."

Seemingly unafraid of heights, Dora climbed over ledge after ledge like a mountain goat, while the trek left Amalia nervous, cold, and hungry. When the older woman finally turned back down the mountain, Amalia breathed a sigh of relief and eagerly followed, carefully watching each step and silently praying that Onkel Andreas would have a warm fire waiting when they returned.

The path down the mountain was steep and treacherous. It eventually twisted past a waterfall, crossed a creek, and wound its way toward a tiny lake. As they neared the Alpenhaus, they passed several tan and white cows lounging in a bed of early clover. The creatures stared at the intruders with mild interest, lazily chewing their cud.

Amalia was beginning to realize just how exhausting it was to gather herbs—even before any drying, soaking, or preserving took place. She was already thinking this wasn't a path she planned to follow.

Her reason for coming to the highlands was to see Peter, or at least to hear about him. But so far, his mother hadn't mentioned his name, and Amalia had been careful not to ask.

It was still early spring, but with the unusually warm weather, she wondered if he had already gone traveling.

Still, she couldn't help hoping that he might show up.

5 Cabin

The Alpenhaus looked as worn down by the winds as Amalia felt. It appeared to have undergone several changes through the centuries. The back half was made from mountain rocks, while the newer front section—if any of it could be called new—was formed from dark, square, and rough-hewn timbers. The back half was built into the earth as if it were trying to escape from the elements. Swinging from the low eaves hung several bundles of drying herbs and buckets of sap that Amalia had helped gather earlier in the day.

It was a delightful summer place with plenty of room to dry herbs and make loaves of cheese before bringing them down to the valley to cure, but Amalia wondered how harsh the winters might be at such an altitude. The window was tiny, and the only doorway was short. Even Amalia, though she was small, had to duck to avoid hitting her head.

Once inside, the room opened to a higher ceiling. As her eyes adjusted to the darker room, she saw a long worksta-

tion for preparing food and making cheese, with a dining area centered around a large rock fireplace. Amalia
noticed the wooden table and chairs were hand-carved.
There was also a couple of feather ticks in the corner,
and a wooden rocking chair next to the fire. Dora proud-
ly pointed to another doorway at the back of the room.
She explained that it was a smaller sleeping room with a
bed, and behind that was a long root cellar that went so
far into the earth that it doubled the size of the building.

Amalia gratefully stretched her frozen hands toward
the crackling fire. A pot of bubbling stew hung over it,
suspended from a rod. Her stomach growled as she got
a whiff of its savory aroma.

Dora reached over to look inside the pot and stir it.

Onkel Andreas came out of the back room. "I added
some barley and onion to the stew. I hope you don't
mind."

Dora laughed. "Mind? Your stew is as good as mine,
Onkel." She put her arm around the older man in a loving
embrace.

As soon as she regained the circulation in her fingers,
Amalia tugged on her cap, allowing her long chestnut
braids to fall to her waist, and free her head from its
weight. That summer, she would be celebrating her four-
teenth birthday and she prayed her mother would allow
her to start wearing her hair up. Meanwhile, she hoped
the Britt family would view her as a young woman and
not as a mere child.

She turned her head at a sound behind her, and was pleased to see Peter ducking through the door, with an armload of dandelion greens.

His father followed behind with a handful of garlic leaves. "It's too early in the season for berries, but the greens seem to be thriving." Jakob Britt set the leaves on the table.

Amalia blushed when Peter smiled at her.

"Guten tag, Amalia, did you enjoy the hike up to the cliffs?"

Amalia lowered her head before smiling back. "Ja, it was beautiful, but cold."

As the family gathered around the table, Onkel Andreas handed Amalia a hand-carved wooden bowl filled with stew.

Dora sliced some cheese and sausage while Jakob Britt brought a basket of apples from the back room. He offered one to Amalia. "Last apples in the storeroom. I hope we have a better harvest this year."

Amalia accepted the fruit with a smile. The meal was a feast at a time when many of their friends had little to eat.

While the family ate, Onkel Andreas ignored his supper and told them a story.

"A man owned a silver mine that had once shown great promise, but it became harder and harder to find any silver as the years went by. After working it for years and gaining so little profit, he resented his investment and decided to shut down the operation."

"One day, he met a stranger who owned a slate mine. The man explained how people all over Europe and even

America were buying slate to make chalkboards for schools and businesses. They even had a market for small slates so children could use them in school to learn their reading and arithmetic."

"After his encounter with this stranger, the man who had expended nearly everything he owned to get silver, remembered seeing slate in his mine. He went back to look, and sure enough—he owned a slate mine. He opened it back up, and soon became wealthy."

Onkel Andreas stopped to look at Peter with a convincing expression. "I'm telling you this, young man, because chasing one dream can sometimes keep us from realizing what we already have. If you ever own a mine, make sure you know what type of mine it is."

Peter laughed. "Thank you, Onkel. I'll keep that in mind, but I'm not planning to own any mines—I'm an artist."

His uncle winked. "Well, in that case, make sure you know what type of artist you want to be."

Everyone laughed, and then Jakob Britt took his turn telling Amalia how he discovered that he was a furniture maker.

"It seems every year something goes wrong with the crops. One year, it was a fire caused by those darn foehn winds, the following year, we had so little sun nothing grew, and then we had a drought. I was weary of farming and needed something for my hands to do during the long winters, so I decided to start carving furniture."

Dora's face glowed with pride. "And his hard work is beginning to pay off. His furniture has started to make its way into some of the finest homes of Glarus."

Peter looked as proud of his father as his mother sounded. "Hey Vater, don't forget to tell her how you survived as a soldier—when you fought against Napoleon."

Onkel Andreas chuckled, "I think I helped Jakob become a good fighter. We certainly argued enough when he was young."

"That's because you tried to keep me from marrying your niece. Just think how lonely you'd be tonight if I hadn't."

Laughter filled the room, and Amalia recognized it as the same infectious, deep belly laugh that attracted her to Peter when they were down by the lake. Although her own family was polite and quiet, she liked these people who worked hard and laughed freely.

When the meal was over, Amalia jumped up to clear the dishes. She was getting ready to wash them in the tub when Dora waved her away.

"Jakob and I will spend the night up here, and Peter will walk you home. You should head back before your father worries about you."

Amalia's heart skipped. This was her chance to learn more about Peter. As they started down the mountain, she tried to think of something to say.

"Which do you like better—living on the farm or up at the Alpenhaus?"

"Both. I love nature and growing things, but I plan to make my living by painting portraits. An artist must go where the people are."

"Vater says very few people around here can afford portraits." After she spoke, Amalia hoped she didn't sound pessimistic about his work.

"That's why I travel through Germany and France. All a man needs to do in the city is set up an easel, and the wealthy will stand in line."

"Don't you enjoy living in Switzerland?"

"Of course! This is my home. I travel just enough to earn money and bring back supplies."

Amalia nodded. She admired his confidence. Peter seemed like a young man who knew what he wanted.

When Peter's eyes nervously shifted to the side of the trail, Amalia's neck grew tense. Was there a wild animal pursuing them? A wolf or a lynx? She'd heard of a child who was killed by a lynx when her mother was young.

Her eyes darted from side to side, scanning the bushes—until she realized Peter wasn't looking for wild animals at all—he had something else on his mind.

"I'd like to draw your face, would you sit for me?"

Amalia smiled. "Sure, as long as Vater agrees."

Their conversation flowed much easier than that night on the dock. They spoke of art and cows and growing things. Before Amalia realized it, they were already in the village, nearing her house.

Peter stopped walking as they entered Herr Kubli's pear orchard. His eyes gazed into hers, and Amalia felt her heart beating faster as she waited for him to speak. Slowly, his hand reached toward her left ear and pulled a pear blossom from her hair. That's when she noticed a blossom in his hair, too, and then she saw another and another. They both looked up to see white blossoms floating through the air all around them.

Amalia laughed. "It's snowing!"

Peter remained silent as he gently leaned over and touched his lips to hers. Amalia felt her face growing hot as she looked around to make sure nobody saw the affectionate gesture, but there was no one. Just the two of them in the orchard, surrounded by the glorious scent of spring.

Once Peter left, Amalia stood on the porch to regain her composure before entering the house. Her parents sat on each side of the fireplace as they always did. Maria was working on her embroidery, while Herr Grob read aloud from the Bible. Amalia waited reverently until he finished before she spoke.

"Vater, Peter Britt has asked if he can draw my likeness. Would you approve?"

Herr Grob sighed, then he looked up from the Good Book with a stern expression. Whenever he frowned, his eyebrows grew into one. "Well Mousekin, what do you think?"

Amalia rolled her eyes to hear him using her childhood name. Her mother once explained how her father thought she had ears like a little mouse when she was born. As his firstborn and the apple of his eye, Herr Grob couldn't resist giving his daughter a pet name.

Fearing his concern, Amalia tried to make the request sound as casual as possible. "It might be interesting to see if his drawing is a good likeness."

"I won't stop you from sitting for him, but I hope you realize that a young man like Peter Britt will probably want to draw every girl in the village."

Amalia nodded to her father, before bidding her parents goodnight and climbing the stairs. She couldn't wait to be alone with her thoughts.

Turning down the duvet, she reflected on the day's events. She wasn't sure if she wanted to become a healer, but she'd accomplished her goal to spend time with Peter. She shivered with delight at the memory of his lips touching hers. Ursula or any other girl in the village would be jealous if they knew. As she dozed off, Amalia smiled at the memory of Peter staring into her eyes while pear blossoms danced around them, landing on his dark hair. It seems he'd found her face as fascinating as she'd found his.

6 Artist

"Maria! Come here!" Herr Grob's voice sounded irritated.

Amalia sighed as she looked at herself in the mirror. She was glad she had plans to leave the house. There was nothing she dreaded more than dealing with her father when he was in a bad mood.

"Where's the coffee?"

Maria set the pitcher of cream on the table. "We've run out."

"I don't like this barley beverage. It might look like coffee, but it does nothing to wake a man up."

"I'm sorry, dear, but Herr Müller says there's not a single bean left in the village."

"Again? Why can't he keep it in stock?"

"He thought he had a decent reserve for the winter, but some rich merchant from Glarus Town came along and offered him a price he couldn't refuse."

"I guess that's how it is these days—whoever has the most, gets the goods. It's not fair."

"I was hoping to get more flour and sugar, too. But those luxuries are hard to find."

Herr Grob shook his napkin to unfold it. "Luxuries? Seems like basic necessities to me. Every year it gets worse. We need these items to get us through the winter."

"Tell me about it, I barely have enough flour to make a loaf of *birnbrot*."

In the Linth Valley, coffee, flour, and sugar were always in short supply. Although they were staples of Glarner kitchens, they had to be imported, which made them expensive and hard to find. Glarus didn't have a long enough growing season for wheat, while sugar and coffee came from faraway places like South America. As a result, all three commodities were often reserved for those with means.

Struggling to make do with what they had was a common frustration for the Glarner women, who constantly stretched every cup of flour and grain of sugar. One solution was to make birnbrot, or pear bread. It was a loaf made from minced dried pears, nuts, and raisins, all packed into a pastry shell with aromatic spices and baked into a round loaf. Once cooled, Birnbrot could be sliced and served like bread. It was especially tasty with cheese.

Ignoring her parents' discussion, Amalia studied her face in the mirror and smiled with satisfaction. She looked forward to spending time with Peter while he drew her picture. Pulling her braids to one side, she tied them together with a bow and tucked them over her shoulder, as far out of the way as possible. It was the best she could do since she couldn't yet wear her hair up. After straightening the white scarf at her throat, she placed a blue bonnet on her head. Most Glarner women wore the head covering. Satisfied that she looked like a mature woman from the front, she pinched both cheeks vigorously before stepping out the door.

It was encouraging to hear her mother's friends say how grown up she was, but she felt annoyed whenever they discussed men for her to marry. Did they expect her to marry some homely, boring old man who wanted her to cook his meals, and bear his children? No, thank you. If she was going to find a match, it must be for love. Anything else was out of the question as far as Amalia was concerned.

Peter suggested they meet on Saturday afternoon under the pine tree at the church. Herr Grob had approved the place since it was out in the open, and there would be no question of what they were doing. But as she grew closer to the church, Amalia saw the crowd and realized her father was right. Peter must have invited everyone in the village—even worse, every girl in Obstalden seemed to want Peter to draw her picture.

Disgusted by the thought of so many girls flirting and jostling for Peter's attention, Amalia turned to go back home. She'd only gone a few steps before bumping into Ursula.

If there was anyone she wanted to avoid, it was Ursula, but it seemed impossible in such a small community. The two girls had once been friends, but as they grew older, they competed for the best grades and the friendships of other girls. The thought of Ursula trying to gain Peter's affection irritated Amalia so much that she decided to stay after all.

She got in line just in time to hear Peter explaining his purpose to the crowd.

"I'm working on two projects—drawings for my portfolio and money for my education. I'm planning to go to art school in Munich. You can sit for a drawing, and if you'd like to keep it, you can pay a small sum. If not, I'll add it to my collection."

With such a long line, Amalia figured it would take hours before Peter got to her and Ursula, who stood at the back of the line. As usual, Ursula asked nosy questions while Amalia tried to give her the shortest answers possible. It was a game they'd been playing for years.

"Did you know our friend Helen is getting married?"

"Yes."

"I think Peter's rather handsome, don't you?"

"I guess."

After several friendly attempts to start a conversation, Ursula grew irritated, "Come on, Amalia, why must you keep avoiding me?"

"What do you want me to say?"

"Say it's been six years. Just say you miss her—say you're sorry we can't have fun like we did when she was still here."

Amalia turned away. She was sorry—sorrier than anyone knew—but she didn't want to remember how her cousin Barbara had died when they were eight. It was too much to think about on such a beautiful day.

She felt relieved to step toward Peter when it was finally her turn, but Ursula, angry at being ignored, pushed in front of her.

Peter shook his head. "I believe Amalia is next."

Amalia sat down on the rock Peter was using as a chair. There was still a crowd standing around to watch the artist at work. Amalia hated to be the center of attention, but she was determined to ignore the mixed feelings churning inside her and gave him her best smile. Peter flashed her a quick grin before his gaze turned serious, and then he began to sketch in silence. It seemed he was taking longer with her picture than he had with the others.

The only sound Amalia could hear was the pencil scratching the tablet until a bearded vulture called overhead. Despite the strain on her facial muscles, she kept her smile frozen. She was hoping for a beautiful portrait.

When Peter finished, she heard gasps and several positive comments from the crowd. Curious, she leaned forward to see for herself. It was an excellent likeness. Perhaps it would soften her father's heart toward Peter. She decided to put a coin in the basket and keep it.

"No wonder her picture looks so good—you spent twice as long drawing her as everyone else."

Ursula's tone of voice betrayed her jealousy. Not that she had anything to worry about—she was one of the prettiest girls in the village. Her only flaw was her attitude. Whenever she didn't get her way, she pouted.

As they traded places, Amalia noticed a slight smirk on Peter's face—it was there just for a second, and then it was gone. She wondered what he was thinking. Did he have a secret crush on Ursula? His fingers flew across the tablet as he worked. Did he know her so well that he took no time to draw her? Amalia's heartbeat quickened with jealousy.

Ursula saw the drawing first and shrieked.

An older man in suspenders began to laugh. "Well, look at that! Peter Britt seems to have the ability to draw anyone."

When Peter held the picture up to the crowd, Amalia realized he'd drawn an accurate likeness, but this portrait was different—it revealed Ursula's furrowed brow and pouty lips. Everyone standing nearby had a good laugh, but Ursula was furious.

"Is this what you do? Draw people at their worst so you can make fun of them?" Her face contorted as she tried to avoid her usual pout lest he draw her again.

"If you want a pretty picture, you must bring a pretty face." Peter winked at Amalia.

Then an older woman in the crowd spoke with admiration. "Why, Peter, I imagine you'd like to draw the expressions of the entire village."

Peter smiled. "You're right. Each face and every expression are a challenge for me."

Staring at her picture, Amalia felt strange. Was this all she meant to Peter? Was she just another pretty face to draw?

Ursula spoke again, "I have twin baby sisters at home that might make a great addition to your portfolio."

Peter's eyes lit up with excitement. "That sounds interesting. Can I walk you home?"

Amalia's heart sank. How could she compete with Ursula and her adorable twins?

She searched for something clever to say—but the moment passed. She started to open her mouth to thank him, but Peter was already tucking the drawings into his satchel and following Ursula down the road. Ursula turned just long enough to flash Amalia a victorious smile.

7 Starflower

Amalia woke to a loud knocking at the front door. Sitting up in the dark with a pounding heart, her first thought was that the foehn winds must be back. Was someone's house on fire? Why else would anyone wake them in the middle of the night?

She listened to the conversation as Herr Grob opened the door, but she could only make out the word "child." Thinking it had nothing to do with her, she settled back into bed and pulled the duvet over her shoulder.

She was drifting back to sleep when she heard a second knock—this time, on her bedroom door. Crawling out of bed in a disoriented state, she opened the door to find Herr Grob standing in his nightshirt, with a candlestick in one hand.

"Amalia, get dressed and come downstairs. Dora Britt is up on the mountain, and Herr Kamm's child has taken ill with a fever. I'll wait here with the candle."

She turned back into her room and quickly threw on a dress, before following her father down the narrow stairway into the kitchen.

Opening a cupboard, she searched through the apothecary bottles until she found the powdered willow bark. She stirred some into water and honey, then poured the mixture into a small vial.

Handing the medicine to the young father, she instructed him. "Place a drop on the tip of her tongue every three hours. And remember to keep wiping her with a cool cloth—but don't allow her to get chilled."

The worried father gave a frantic nod before dashing back into the night.

Herr Grob handed the candle to his daughter, then muttering under his breath about a man not being able to get sleep in his own home, he opened the door to the downstairs bedroom, while Amalia carried the candle back up the stairs.

Her mind was spinning with concern. Had she done the right thing? Would the remedy help? What if they gave the child too much? Would she be responsible if a child died? Perhaps she should've gone with the man—but she had little experience dealing with sick children. Many of the villagers knew she'd been working with Dora Britt, but this was the first time someone had come to ask for her help. Despite being awakened in the middle of the night, Amalia felt good about the opportunity to help others and be recognized for it.

Over a year had passed since Amalia first climbed the mountain. Hot foehn winds had come again and gone. They continued to terrorize the Linth Valley. Famine and sickness had also plagued the community. There was always a demand for Dora's cures. Amalia had grown accustomed to climbing the mountain, gathering herbs, and preparing potions by now. There were weeks when she spent so much time up on the mountain, that Herr Grob teased his daughter with a new nickname, "mountain goat."

The apprenticeship was hard work, but she enjoyed learning about homeopathic remedies. Plus, it gave her a little money to help her family buy necessities in hard times. Dora was kind and easy to please. Her stories made Amalia feel closer to Peter—especially when he and Jakob went traveling.

She smiled at how she'd once been afraid of losing Peter to Ursula when he went to draw the twins. Within a month, she ran into him at the Alpenhaus, and they picked up where they left off. Peter was always wanting to draw her face and telling her stories of his travels, while she was always eager to listen.

Amalia noted the differences between her family and Peter's. While her family had a larger house and a more stable income, the Britts had the uncanny ability to adapt and use whatever resources they found in nature, to make life better for themselves and others. The Britt home in the village displayed beautiful furniture usually seen in much wealthier homes—yet each piece had been hand-carved by Jakob. The vegetables they ate came from Dora's garden, and were often seasoned with the delicious *Schabziger* cheese made by Kaspar and Onkel Andreas at the Alpenhaus. Most locals grated the hard, greenish cheese over their food as a household staple.

Even though the Britt family utilized their creativity at every opportunity, even they were no match for the foehn winds. Those horrible hot winds continued to ruin their crops—leaving them without stone fruit one year and causing great losses of hay and other harvests, in others. To make ends meet, Jakob and Peter traveled for months at a time throughout Europe, making oil portraits for the wealthy.

Amalia wasn't surprised to learn that Peter's father could paint portraits too. After all, he was the one who taught Peter—but his son had developed his own style. Each painting included an object of importance to reveal the subject's character—a technique that guaranteed happy customers wherever he went.

The perks of traveling in other countries included bringing back exotic woods for Jakob's carving, along with flour, sugar, and coffee—which could be traded with the Glarner people. The Britts weren't wealthy, but they made the best of what they had. Their life was filled with music, art, food, love, and laughter. Amalia admired each of them for their gifts and knew that any woman would be fortunate to join such a family. And she secretly hoped that woman would be her.

One afternoon, Amalia was helping Dora harvest herbs in the meadow near the Alpenhaus when she looked up to find Peter smiling down at her. Her heart fluttered with excitement to know he was back in the canton.

"My mutter must be grateful for your help. Her knees are worn out from years of crawling on the meadow floor."

Amalia gathered her apron full of herbs and stood up. "I'm glad to help!"

Peter held out a white, star-shaped flower. "I found this on the trail."

Dora, who was collecting on the far side of the meadow, rushed over to hug her son. Noticing the white flower, she smiled. "Ah! My French neighbor calls this the alpine star."

Amalia studied the soft plant. Tiny yellow flowers were surrounded by white, woolly leaves arranged in the shape of a star.

Dora continued her lesson. "It's good for so many things. Some use it as a smudge to ward off evil spirits. Onkel Andreas swears it heals cow udders, and it's especially good for consumption and stomach trouble. Dry it and add it to your tea—I think you'll find it's a good tonic for those headaches that come with the foehn winds."

Smiling gratefully at Peter, Amalia tucked the star flower in with the herbs before carrying them to the cabin.

Amalia lingered long past the time her family expected her to be home. She wanted to hear every story Peter had to tell of his journey, but eventually, she had to go—or face her father's questions. By then, Amalia knew the path well, so she bid the Britts goodnight and made the trek down the mountain alone.

She was just coming to the gate when she met Ursula.

"I've been going door to door, collecting clothing for the Zwicki family, whose house burned last week." Ursula looked at her with anticipation—clearly expecting Amalia to donate.

Realizing the quickest way to get Ursula out of the house would be to find a dress she no longer wore, Amalia led the other girl into the kitchen. She set the starflower on the table before rushing upstairs.

When she returned, Ursula was cradling the starflower in her hands as if it were a sign from God.

"Where'd you get this?"

"Peter gave it to me." She felt a small victory in saying those words.

Ursula was quiet and seemed more thoughtful than usual as she fingered the soft petals. Was she upset—or jealous? Amalia tried to break the tension between them.

"Some call it *edelweiss*, but I think starflower is a prettier name."

"It's a sign that Peter would risk his life for you," Ursula blurted out. Amalia thought she said it just a little too loud.

Hoping Herr Grob, who was reading the Glarus Newspaper in the parlor wouldn't hear them, Amalia lowered her voice to a whisper. "What are you talking about?"

"The legend of the starflower—haven't you heard it?"

Amalia shook her head.

"There's an old legend that says a man who climbs to the highest precipice on the mountain to get the starflower truly loves the woman he gives it to—because he was willing to risk his life to get it."

From the other room they could hear Herr Grob snort. "That's just a made-up tale so some man can look brave. The truth is, you can find starflowers even in the meadows."

Amalia ignored her father's outburst and changed the subject. She preferred to discuss the plant's virtues, rather than Peter's, in front of her father.

"They say it has magical healing powers because it can survive in the most extreme cold at the highest elevations."

Ursula folded the dress Amalia gave her and stacked it on the others. "I believe it."

Once Ursula was gone, Amalia wondered what to do with the flower.

If she pressed it in the family Bible, her father might worry that she was sentimental about Peter. Herr Grob was a practical man who had little time for romantic notions.

If she combined it with other herbs and steeped it in her special tea, as Dora suggested, her father wouldn't suspect anything.

Amalia pondered her feelings. The flower didn't matter as much as the love she'd seen in Peter's eyes that afternoon. Her heart felt warm at the memory of it.

When a friend of Herr Grob's knocked on the front door, Amalia stepped into her father's office. Once she found the family Bible, it only took a moment to decide where to press it. In the tradition of Zwingli, the Reformed pastor who once lived in Glarus, Herr Grob always read from the Gospels. She slipped the flower into Psalm 23, which as far as her father was concerned, was just a sentimental poem.

A week later, Amalia came back to claim her prize. If Herr Grob noticed the starflower in the Bible, he never mentioned it. Taking the now dried flower upstairs, she placed it in her secret box and tucked it under her bed.

Whenever she thought about the legend of the starflower, Amalia smiled. Even if it wasn't true, she liked to believe that Peter Britt would be willing to risk his life for her.

8 Gatherings

Obstalden, Glarus, 1842

Amalia reached behind the loose stone in the wall. Was the space empty? Or would she find something hiding there? She remembered the year her father built the barrier around their house and garden. Herr Grob had rejected this rock because it fit awkwardly due to its odd shape, leaving an open gap behind it. Six-year-old Amalia had insisted he keep it so she and her friends could use it as a secret hiding place. Throughout childhood, the only other people who knew about it were Ursula and her cousin Barbara. The three friends had used the space to hide ribbons, stones, feathers, and secret notes about boys they had a crush on.

Years later, when Amalia showed Peter the moveable rock, he put it to good use. While he was traveling, she checked it daily. If Peter passed by in the night or too early to knock on the Grob family door, he left some little gift to let her know that he was back in the canton. She never knew what she might find behind the stone—a love poem, a flower, or some trinket he'd found in his travels.

When her fingers felt the soft, cool petals of an Alpenrose, she smiled and pulled out the bright pink flower with satisfaction. Carefully slipping the stone back in place, she ran back inside the house to check her appearance in the mirror.

A stray tendril hung from the braid on top of her head. She quickly tucked it into place and pulled the flower's bell-shaped sections apart, sliding one bloom into her braid. Turning her head, she admired the flower's effect before vigorously pinching both cheeks seven times. She hoped the color would remain until she saw Peter. Then she raced out the door to choir practice.

Further down the road, Herr Grob had finished work for the day and was stepping into the tavern with a group of men. A rumor had spread around the village that the men had something important to discuss, but Amalia couldn't imagine anything more important than seeing Peter. In her rush through the village, she nearly collided with Jakob Britt. He gave her a fatherly smile as they passed in opposite directions.

Seven years had come and gone since Kaspar and Anna's wedding. The young teenagers who sat by the Walensee that dark, starry night had grown. Amalia was a beautiful twenty-year-old woman whose body now filled out her dress, while twenty-three-year-old Peter had finally grown a full beard. Most girls in the village assumed that Peter was planning to marry Amalia. Even Ursula seemed to have given up on him as a potential suitor.

Amalia entered the church to discover that the choir director had already called for the singers to take their places. Her eyes searched the room until she found Peter waving to her from the other side of the choir loft with a big smile. She wished she could run over and throw her arms around him, but it wouldn't be proper. They'd need to wait for a private moment to show their affection.

It was exciting to hear Peter's voice harmonizing with hers, even if she couldn't touch him. As they practiced a lively anthem, Amalia felt like a great wind had filled her lungs, and she could sing higher than usual. When Peter's eyes met hers, she imagined the angels in heaven must be singing with them.

She was still fascinated with him, but Peter's life was no longer mysterious. During his travels throughout Europe, he kept in touch by sending letters full of drawings and stories from the places he visited. Their friendship had become intimate throughout the changing seasons, and they'd grown to know each other quite well—much to Herr Grob's dismay.

Despite what the villagers thought, Peter and Amalia still had a significant obstacle to overcome—they needed Herr Grob's blessing. They were desperately in love, but it was against the law for a woman in the canton to marry without her father's approval. Amalia felt the law was unfair because it didn't matter how old she got or how much she was in love—her father would always have the last word.

Herr Grob made it no secret that he did not support Amalia's affections for Peter. He often rolled his eyes when she received a letter and constantly warned her to keep her options open. It wasn't that he didn't like Peter—he just desired a better match. He wanted his daughter to have a husband who stayed in the canton—not a wanderer who made his living on the streets of foreign cities.

Herr Grob had one goal—for Amalia to marry a man who could provide for her. Amalia also had one goal—to marry for love. She understood her father's concerns, but she felt he was overlooking Peter's steadfast character. Even at twenty, she was in no hurry to get married. She reveled in Peter's attention—especially when her father's back was turned.

Amalia had many things to tell Peter that summer evening, but the short walk home wasn't long enough to share everything in her heart. Peter had stories of his own. In their haste to speak, they both began talking at the same time—then laughed. A moment later, they interrupted each other again.

Once they reached the porch, Peter reached for her hand. Amalia nervously glanced around, wary of gossiping neighbors, but on this balmy summer night, it felt like they were the only people in the world.

After another traveler's tale, Peter yawned. "Well, my darling, I'm happy to see your face, but I need some sleep after my long journey. I'll see you tomorrow and catch up some more."

Amalia nodded. "I'm glad you're home safe."

Peter leaned over to kiss her hand. "When we have a daughter, I hope she's exactly like you!"

"With my *Mousekin* ears?"

He smiled in that adoring way that always warmed her heart.

"I hope she has your good character and delightful personality—and that she loves to sing and hike the trails with me."

Long after she went inside, Amalia couldn't stop smiling. It felt good to be loved for being herself. She went to sleep, dreaming about becoming a wife and mother.

Down the road, the men in the tavern were having a heated discussion. While their young people had enjoyed an evening of singing, flirting, and making future plans, the elders wore grave faces.

A man named Brunner opened the meeting by announcing that the future of Obstalden—and the entire canton—was at stake. Those listening were all too familiar with the situation.

"This past decade has not been kind to the canton. Foehn winds, sickness, and famine have followed in succession, as if attempting to wipe the Glarner people from the face of the earth. Besides the agricultural losses, the garment industry has been hit hard by newly built factories, which have put nearly 2,000 people out of work who were making their living by spinning material at home."

The group of men groaned. Such dismal conditions had etched the wrinkles deeper into Herr Grob's face. He, like many fathers in Glarus, was worried about his children's future.

Brunner cleared his throat and began reading from the *Schwanden* newspaper, where they were starting something called "The Glarus Emigration Society."

"The goal of the organization is to buy land in America and send people to farm it, in exchange for giving them the land if they stay for a certain length of time. This will both lessen the stress on the local economy and give those willing to leave a new start."

Brunner had barely finished reading the announcement before the room erupted in shouting. Migration was a volatile topic, and everyone had an opinion. Relatives and friends found themselves divided. Some thought leaving their homeland was a moral defeat, while others felt they might have no choice. The future of the canton was at stake, and the arguments grew louder as the evening wore on.

A small man with a long beard climbed onto a chair to be seen. "It's the factories that are at fault—they've stolen the jobs of our people."

A dark-haired man countered with his opinion. "The factories have indeed replaced some jobs, but that's progress. It's those damn foehn winds that are the real problem."

A large man in the back of the room, who looked as if he'd never missed a meal in his life, stood up. "Hear, hear! There's more than one way to look at this situation. We have many poor people among us who are not ambitious. If we can send them to a place where they'll find more work opportunities, they might better themselves—and we'll have more food for those left behind."

Another farmer agreed. "We already have more hungry people in the canton than we have food. Perhaps emigration is a wise solution. Sending people to America will lighten the load for everyone."

From there, it became a shouting match.

"Hunger is the problem. They're already placing guards at the gardens to make sure no one harvests their potatoes before they are full-grown—we may need every bite to make it through the winter."

"That's ridiculous! People should be allowed to harvest their garden whenever they want."

"But the larger the potato, the more mouths it will feed."

"Make sure no one steals what isn't theirs."

"Some people are just lazy! They place a burden on the rest of us to help them—let them go!"

"If an eagle flew over Glarus, he'd find the Glarner people are thrifty. Nearly every corner of our yards is taken up in gardens or orchards."

"'Tis the mountains that have crowded out our fields and left us with nowhere to grow wheat, so we must buy our grains from other places."

"Perhaps we should all seek a flatter land."

"But who is willing to go? Shall we rip the flag in two and carry one half to America?"

"Just because a man's crops have failed doesn't mean he's lazy. No one but God can control those damn foehn winds."

This last man spoke the truth, and many of the men knew it. Whether from admission or defeat, they lowered their voices.

The older man continued. "Look, men, we're faced with a dilemma. Growing crops is necessary—it's the only way to feed our families. And America has plenty of land to grow many crops. This seems to be a viable solution."

"But at what price? Must we sacrifice our homeland and friends to survive?" Herr Grob shook his head in despair. "Shall we send our children and grandchildren across the ocean to never see them again? God forbid!"

After listening all evening, Jakob Britt finally spoke. "Anyone who travels with the help of the Glarus Emigration Society should consider that they might be beholden to do as the society tells them. If I went to America, I'd be sure to pay my own way."

"You? Go to America? What is this, Britt? Since when did you start talking about going to America?" Herr Grob didn't like the sound of it. He hoped such nonsense wouldn't rub off on Peter and Amalia.

"Since I've begun to realize there are opportunities in America that our children and grandchildren might never find here in Glarus."

"Oh, twaddle! Our children are Swiss-born, and they belong here. They'll find a way to survive just like our ancestors have for generations."

"Will they? The famines have stolen our crops for three of the last five years. My Peter and I have been forced to travel and paint portraits to keep our family clothed and fed. It is these damn foehn winds—when will they ever end? If America has no wind, it must be paradise."

"But Switzerland is our home. Going to America will only steal our children and make them Americans. What will become of our beloved homeland?"

"And what good will it do to stay if our grandchildren starve?"

"Stop this nonsense! We must find a way to stay." Herr Grob slammed his fist on the table for emphasis.

As Jakob Britt rose to leave, he leaned over to have the last word. "If we stay, we may end up eating each other."

9 Alpabzug

WHEN AMALIA WOKE TO the smell of sausage and potatoes frying, she tried to remember where she was. Rolling over in the dim light, she recognized Kaspar's wife, Anna, and her baby lying beside her on a feather tick. Then she remembered she was at the Alpenhaus, and Dora must be cooking breakfast. It seemed too early to eat, but that was the farmer's life. Onkel Andreas was known for getting up while it was still dark outside. Amalia rolled over to get a little more sleep.

Off in the distance, she could hear yodeling. It was intriguing to hear the Britt men communicate across the alpine landscape as their ancestors had. Amalia smiled as the sweet harmonies gently soothed her back to sleep like a faint lullaby.

Then her eyes flew open, as she sat up straight. It was *Alpabzug*—if the men were already rounding up the cows, there was no time to sleep. She jumped up and went to the pitcher to splash icy water on her face.

One glance at the clock confirmed her suspicions that it was early—only three in the morning. Dora's cheerful "*Guten Morgen*" seemed a little too cheerful for such an early hour, but Amalia mumbled a polite reply as she poured herself a cup of coffee.

Alpabzug, or alpine descent, was the day in September when the farmers brought the cows home from the higher pastures. On this day, cows were celebrated as an essential part of Glarus life. A good family cow could provide milk for the children and cheese for the table. Most people could afford only one or two cows, so they sent their cows to be boarded on the higher pastures by those like Onkel Andreas, who farmed for a living.

Life at the Alpenhaus revolved around the cows. Dairy farming was a multi-generational business, handed down from father to son. The farmer's tasks included milking the cows, making the cheese, and bringing it down from the mountain to age for a year.

Like his ancestors, Onkel Andreas knew every trick of the trade. He knew how to use blue clover to make the most delicious cheese, but he could also burn a starflower smudge to heal an infected udder—or turn a breech calf inside the womb.

Since she was a child, Amalia had enjoyed the festival, but this was her first time participating with the farmers. The day before, she'd helped Dora fill a cart with gentians, asters, ferns, and moss to create nine floral wreaths for the cows to wear on their way home. The wreaths, tied with ribbons and embroidered neckbands, formed elaborate headgear to place on each cow. From each cow's neck hung a large bell to ward off evil spirits for the coming year.

It was still dark when the men came inside for breakfast. By then, Anna was up and pouring milk for the sleepy-eyed children while the family gathered around the table to discuss the day's plans.

"Who wants to take charge of the bull?"

"I'll do it," Peter volunteered then leaned over to whisper in Amalia's ear. "I'll need to keep the bull separate from the cows on the way down, but we'll have the rest of the day together."

"I'll take the cheese cart." Jakob scooped up his last forkful of potatoes, then chugged his coffee as if he were in a hurry.

Like most farmers, Onkel Andreas made cheese at the Alpenhaus all summer, then took the uncured cheese down with the cows in the fall. Back in Obstalden, the fresh cheese would exchange places with last year's cured loaves, which were ready for the dinner table.

Amalia helped wash the dishes before following Dora outside to dress the cows. By then, the small pond near the Alpenhaus had turned pink, while the barn, trees, and cattle remained dark silhouettes against the ever-brightening sky.

Dora pushed the cart full of wreaths over to the cows and stopped in front of the first one. "This is Ella. She's easy to dress, but the younger ones might be more stubborn."

She showed Amalia how to tie the floral crown onto Ella's head. Ella mooed and excitedly shifted her weight when

Peter placed a large bell around her neck and secured the buckle.

Amalia adjusted a daisy on the wreath before standing back to admire her work. "She looks beautiful."

Dora nodded, "She's earned the right to be queen for the day. She gives us lots of good milk." Dora patted the cow with affection before turning back to the wreaths. "One down, eight more to go!"

When they had decorated the last cow, they looked like nine bovine brides waiting to meet their groom at the altar. Of course, there was just the one groom who needed extra monitoring to ensure he behaved. Because of this, Peter had already left to find the bull.

Under the direction of Onkel Andreas, Jakob and Kaspar loaded stacks of round cheese from the storeroom onto the cart. They would take turns pushing the cart down to the village while prodding the cattle from behind.

Ready to start the descent, the family members spread out on all sides, surrounding the cows, waiting for Onkel Andreas to give the word.

No one said it aloud, but Onkel Andreas had been unwell all summer. Amalia could tell from the looks Dora and Jakob exchanged that they feared this might be his last descent and they wanted everything to please the old cattleman.

Just as the sun peeked over the Alps, the Britt family finally began their descent, with Onkel Andreas leading the way while Dora followed, holding the hand of her oldest grandchild. Amalia and Anna, who carried her baby in a sling, walked on each side of the cows. Kaspar and Jakob followed behind with the cart, ready to prod any wanderers at the back. And then, much farther behind, Peter guided the bull from the rear.

Amalia usually walked quickly from the Alpenhaus to the village, but herding the cattle took time. The goal was to keep the cows plodding along and guide any strays back onto the trail and away from the cliffs. Onkel Andreas had given her the task of watching an obstinate heifer named Lena. She hoped she was up to the task. The trail was steep, and a young calf could easily frolic over the edge.

As the day wore on, they met other farmers leading their cows down. Each herd fell in behind another until they formed one long parade. The closer they got to home, the faster the cows walked. By the time they neared the village, some of the cows were running.

Alpabzug was a high day for the Glarner people. The constant clanging of the bells signaled the cows' descent long before they came into view, and people from the surrounding villages lined up along the route to watch them return before rushing into the day's festivities.

Amalia breathed a sigh of relief when all the cows had made it down safely. Unsure where Peter was, she ran home to tidy her hair. She was done playing farmer and wanted to look her best. Smoothing the top of her head, she tucked a purple aster into the braid, hoping it would remain fresh during the busy day ahead.

Amalia had planned to slip back out the door, hoping no one would see her, but Herr Grob called to her from his study.

"Yes, Vater?"

"Ah, good to see you back. Did you enjoy the descent?"

"Yes, Vater." She shifted from one foot to the other, eager to find Peter.

"I hope you remember that you're still young, *Mousekin*. This is your time to have many suitors. It's not wise to focus on only one."

"Oh, Vater, Peter's my best friend." Amalia lowered her eyes, lest he think she was disrespectful for expressing her opinion.

Herr Grob twisted his lower lip and slowly rolled his head from side to side, before he patiently replied, "Just promise me you'll keep your mind open to other suitors."

"Yes, Vater."

"And be careful not to do anything that could make potential suitors question your good Christian character."

Amalia rushed out the door with a twinge of guilt, because she had no intention of being with anyone but Peter Britt.

10 Church

Alpabzug was a lively harvest festival that included lots of music. Amalia knew from experience that there would be yodeling contests, choirs, accordions, hammered dulcimers, and finally, the alpine horns would hum a relaxing benediction as the sun slid behind the Alps.

In between all the musical performances, the villagers would barter vegetables, fruit, wine, and cheese—along with hand-crafted items like candles, embroidery, and lace. Children would play games, married couples might dance, and the elders would share their stories of wisdom. It was a high day in Glarus, and Amalia looked forward to sharing it with Peter—if only she could find him.

Once Peter had secured the bull in his pen, he searched the crowd for Amalia and found her waving near the church where they'd agreed to meet. Their choir would be one of the first to sing, so they waited for the others to join them while they practiced a few warm-up notes.

After their choir performed, they wandered through the noisy crowd, trying to hear each other above the music and laughter. Finally, Peter grabbed Amalia's hand and pulled her into the empty church.

"Perhaps we can talk in here without shouting at each other." Peter's eyes seemed to be dancing as he looked over her hair and noted the flower tucked behind her ear.

Amalia stared up at the preaching platform suspended over their heads. "I wonder why the preacher has to be so much higher than everyone else."

Peter's eyes followed hers. "To make him look closer to God than the common people. That's one reason I dislike church."

"Surely you don't mean that."

He shook his head. "I promise you can take our children to church when we have them, but please don't be angry at me for not believing."

Amalia doubted she could ever be mad at Peter—especially when he wore such a mysterious twinkle in his eye. Curious, she turned to face him as she slid closer to him on the wooden pew. There it was again—that confidence mixed with vulnerability in his eyes that had attracted her the first time she saw him down by the Walensee.

She wondered what he was thinking. He seemed to have something to say. It never crossed her mind that he would ever stop loving her—she knew him better than that. No, this was something important, but he sure was taking his time to speak.

Peter cleared his throat. "Amalia, how do you see the future? Do you have any dreams that I don't know about?"

"Well, I'd like to make a better birnbrot, and maybe do more fancy embroidering like my mother."

Peter smiled as he thought about her birnbrot—her version of the spicy bread was among the best he'd ever tasted.

Peter slid down to the floor on his knees. Surprised, Amalia wondered if he was sick or hurt. Perhaps the bull had kicked him, and he hadn't told her. She leaned over with concern to hear what he was about to say.

"Amalia, you've proven that you're capable of many things, from making birnbrot, to herding cattle, to making potions to heal people. I'm not a rich man, but I will do everything within my power to make you happy—if you'll become my wife."

It took a moment to grasp the meaning of his words. Then Amalia's heart began to dance. She sensed he knew her answer already, but she took a moment to drink it in, before throwing her arms around him and giving him a firm "Yes!"

Peter reached into his pocket and pulled out a beautiful silver locket.

Taking it from his hand, Amalia opened it to find a tiny portrait of him inside.

"You can put any picture you want in there. I painted a portrait of your mother, too. Look, it's hidden behind this one."

"Oh, Peter, what a wonderful gift! I've often longed to see your face while you're gone."

Peter smiled. "I don't think I can ever forget your face." Then, making a fist with his hand, he held it over his heart. "I hope you know this man will always hold your heart inside of his own."

Tears filled Amalia's eyes as she threw her arms around him again.

Peter hesitated then asked, "Shall we tell anyone, or should we wait for a while?"

"I can't marry without my father's permission, so we should probably wait a bit. At least until I can convince him."

Peter nodded. "It won't be easy while I'm gone, but it'll be worth it once I make my fortune and build us a home."

Amalia smiled. "Can I borrow your knife?"

Peter pulled the knife from his pocket, while Amalia unraveled a lock of her hair. She wove it into a tiny braid before cutting it free. Twisting the ribbon around it, she tied the lock at both ends, forming a small wreath, and handed it to him.

Peter placed the lock ceremoniously against his lips, before tucking it inside his pocket with the knife. Then he leaned over toward her lips. Amalia glanced nervously around the empty church to make sure no one was watching before she returned his affection.

Amalia marveled at how they were committing their lives to each other inside the church. It was a holy kiss, this trading of gifts, and a promise to love each other forever. She imagined the eyes of God and the holy angels were watching.

Noisy villagers reveled outside, musicians played, and children called out in a game of tag, but the lovers required no one else to celebrate with them, as they quietly planned their future.

Laying her head on Peter's shoulder, Amalia sighed with deep satisfaction. There was no doubt in her mind that Peter was the only man for her. If only she could convince her father of this truth.

Down the road, Herr Grob sat on a bench next to Jakob Britt. Unaware that their families were about to be united, the two men discussed the coming winter and the possibility of better prices for coffee and sugar. Distracted by the lively crowd, Herr Grob had forgotten to keep track of his daughter.

"Say, Britt, look at all those happy cows you brought down from the mountain. Things are looking up—are they not? Perhaps there will be no need to emigrate to America."

Jakob Britt took a swig of beer before answering. "When it comes to the cows, Andreas says it takes a lot of good years to make up for one bad year. The losses of baby calves, milk, and cheese cannot be undone with one good year."

"Yes, but surely it will help."

"I sure hope so."

Long after Peter had walked her home and said good-night, Amalia was too excited to sleep. She finally dozed off with the silver locket in her hand and a smile on her face. In her dreams, she and Peter had a boy and a girl. Fruit trees and plants of every kind surrounded their home. She knew she had chosen the best—no man was more talented or resourceful than Peter Britt.

11 Friends

AMALIA STRUGGLED TO KEEP her engagement a secret. The delicate locket, nestled close to her heart, was both a token of joy and a source of quiet sorrow. What good was happiness if she could not share it openly? She longed to stand atop the Alps and declare her love for Peter Britt to all the world. Yet in the Canton of Glarus, Switzerland, in 1842, a woman could not marry without her father's consent—regardless of her age. Thus, she must bide her time and await the proper moment to persuade him that Peter was indeed the man for her.

The early autumn weather remained warm, and the Britt men were traveling once more. Amalia knew Peter was eager to earn as much as he could before the winter storms set in.

When the latest mail arrived from Germany, Herr Grob waved the letter in front of his daughter.

"I suppose you want to see what your traveling salesman has to say."

Amalia blushed. "Vater, he's an artist—not a traveling salesman."

"Well, let's see. He travels and he sells art. I would call that a traveling salesman."

When she reached for the letter, Herr Grob lifted it higher, teasingly waving it above her head. Knowing better than to argue or struggle, Amalia smiled softly and stood still until he at last handed it to her.

When Herr Grob returned to his office, Amalia turned to her mother.

"Why does Vater refuse to acknowledge anything good about Peter?"

Maria Grob, who was sorting and slicing apples to dry for winter storage, paused to wipe her hands on her apron before replying.

"Perhaps he fears you will fall in love with him."

"Would that be so terrible?"

"He only desires what is best for you."

"But it's not just Peter," Amalia said with a sigh. "He seems displeased with his father, too. I thought you once said he and Jacob Britt had been friends since childhood. Do you think they have quarreled?"

Amalia was counting on their fathers' friendship to strengthen the case for her and Peter to marry.

Maria shook her head. "All this talk about the Glarus Emigration Society has stirred up division—even between old friends."

"I don't understand why."

"Well, it may not be the only reason. Your father is a carpenter from a long line of carpenters, while the Britts come from generations of farmers. For whatever cause, Herr Britt has taken to building furniture. That might explain your father's change in attitude."

"Must the Britts remain farmers simply because their ancestors worked the land for hundreds of years? Shouldn't people be free to better their lot in life?"

Maria sighed as she cut away a bad section of apple.

"With the way this harvest is going, I wouldn't blame any farmer for seeking new ways to earn a living. Some won't have enough food to last the winter. We are fortunate your father has steady work in the good years, enough to set aside for the lean ones."

Amalia's thoughts turned to Ursula, whose father drank Schnapps and had not held steady work in years. His wife was left to shoulder the burden, for he was often drunk. They had welcomed a child nearly every year, and though several had been lost to diphtheria and the fever, seven children still remained to feed. This forced Ursula's mother to spin linen threads to earn a living.

Many Glarner women had taken up spinning to help provide for their families. They worked by the piece, spinning thread from flax stems and selling it to the weaver, who in turn wove it into linen. Though spinning brought in little, it was something. The flax itself was grown by farmers like Jacob Britt. If the Britts were struggling to make ends meet, Amalia wondered, what hope was there for Ursula and her family?

When she had finished helping her mother with the apples, Amalia decided to visit her childhood friend. Upon arriving, she counted at least five children playing in the yard. They wore simple garments of coarse, handspun linen woven from local flax. The twins, now half-grown, regarded her with wary eyes as she knocked on the door.

Ursula, surprised to see her, quickly waved her inside. It had been years since Amalia last entered Ursula's home, and she was taken aback by how cramped it felt. Unwashed dishes cluttered the table, while handmade dolls and worn blankets lay strewn across the floor. A two-year-old wailed at her mother's feet, and from the stench in the room, Amalia guessed the child was in need of changing.

Ursula's mother sat at her spinning wheel near the window, holding flax fibers in one hand while guiding them onto the distaff with the other. She paused briefly to wet her fingers and nod in greeting, then resumed spinning as the wheel clicked steadily on.

Amalia guessed her friend had grown accustomed to the wheel's ceaseless rhythm, though she herself found it distracting. Wishing for a quiet place where they could speak privately, she suggested they go for a walk.

Ursula nodded and glanced toward her baby sister."Just let me change her first."

The fresh air felt like a blessing once they stepped outside. It had been months since their last visit, and Amalia was uncertain how to begin—but Ursula, as always, was never at a loss for words.

Brushing the dirt from her skirt, Ursula laughed. "Please excuse my dress. I've been helping Father Huber collect apple culls from the farmers' fields to give to the poor."

Amalia held her tongue. She couldn't help but think that Ursula's own family would surely be among the first in need of such charity. Yet her friend thought of those who had even less. No matter how often Ursula had exasperated her over the years, Amalia had always admired her generous heart.

The young women had grown apart for several reasons. In their school days, it had been harmless enough—school-girl crushes on boys and rivalry over arithmetic grades. But now, as adults, another, far more divisive issue stood between them—one that reached beyond youthful jealousies.

The Canton of Glarus remained a stronghold of the Swiss Reformed Church, shaped by the legacy of Ulrich Zwingli. Once a Catholic priest, Zwingli had been a contemporary of Martin Luther and preached fervently against the doctrines of the Roman Church. The people of Glarus took pride in the fact that Zwingli himself had once pastored a church in their canton. Through his ministry, he had forever altered the spiritual landscape, carrying the Reformation across all of Switzerland.

Even though the Reformation had taken place several centuries earlier, it still cast a long shadow—one that now drew an invisible line between the two friends. Ursula remained Catholic, while Amalia was Christian Reformed.

Though subtle, such religious differences shaped one's standing in the community. At times, they could influence matters as serious as marriage or the right to run a business. According to the Reformed pastor, Catholics were less spiritual—a claim often repeated from the pulpit and in private conversation. He insisted that anyone could sense the difference the moment they stepped inside a Catholic church.

To the Reformed, Catholics clung to everything Zwingli had denounced and abhorred—from paying for indulgences to worshiping what they called idols. These so-called idols included statues, paintings, and relics of Mary and Jesus.

It was said in certain circles that one could recognize a Catholic by what they wore—especially jewelry, which adorned various parts of the body, from rosaries and crosses to pendants strung around the neck. In contrast, the Christian Reformed dressed plainly and wore no ornaments. Their churches, too, reflected this simplicity—with no pictures, statues, or adornments of any kind.

The debates between Reformed Christians and Catholics had raged centuries earlier, yet the divisions lingered. So few Catholics remained in parts of Glarus that they were sometimes required to share a church building with their Reformed neighbors.

Amalia had grown up keenly aware of these differences. She knew her parents would never approve of her marrying a Catholic—yet marrying a non-believer like Peter at least left room for the hope of conversion.

Burdened by the strict standards of the Reformed Church, Amalia felt she could confide only in a Catholic about the locket hidden beneath her dress, pressed close to her heart.

Out in the fields, far from gossiping ears, Amalia shared the joyful news of her engagement.

Ursula embraced her, though her smile quickly faded.

"How did your Vater take the news?"

Amalia sighed. "He doesn't know. He has little interest in me marrying Peter, and I fear he will oppose it—so I must hide my joy from him. I love Vater, but I cannot live without Peter. Ursula, what am I to do?"

"It will depend on timing," Ursula said gently. "You must wait until your father recognizes Peter's potential as an artist."

Amalia sighed. "I believe you're right. Would you like to see the locket and the portraits he painted?"

Ursula studied the miniature image of Peter, then the one of Maria Grob, and let out a low whistle.

"What a remarkable likeness. And how ingenious—that he made them so you can slip one over the other. It's all so beautiful—I don't know how you'll ever keep it a secret."

She gave a warm smile as she handed the locket back to Amalia.

"I'm glad you recognize his talent. I only hope Vater does."

"Once he sees you're marrying a master, he won't mind that Peter travels for his art," Ursula spoke with quiet confidence.

Amalia hoped she was right.

The young women returned to the house, gossiping about their friends and who else had recently become engaged. For a little while, they forgot their worries and giggled like the schoolgirls they had once been.

A week later, when a second letter arrived, Herr Grob summoned Amalia to his study. Unaware of what had transpired in the church on Alpabzug, he was convinced that victory was within his grasp—if only he could secure his daughter's commitment to another suitor before Peter became serious.

He pulled out a chair, and Amalia sat down, her heart fluttering with apprehension.

"Ah, Amalia, I've been looking forward to this day. Now that you are grown, we can speak about your future."

"What do you mean, Vater?" She frowned, her brow knitting with concern.

"It is time to consider what sort of man we shall choose for your husband."

Amalia sighed. "I am not sure I'm ready."

She knew that was a lie. Of course she was ready—ready to become Peter's wife. But she had grown so accustomed to hiding her true feelings to keep the peace that dishonesty had become second nature. She no longer knew how to break the habit.

"Nonsense." He replied. "You will never be ready if you wait until you feel ready. Marriage is a practical matter—not an emotional quest for love."

12 Suitors

Father and daughter sat across from each other, staring in silence.

Herr Grob had tolerated Amalia's friendship with Peter for years. The Britts were among their closest friends, and the young people had always been proper and respectful. Peter was the model of politeness, and seemed devoted to his daughter, so it had been difficult to forbid their friendship outright. Herr Grob had believed that, if left alone, Amalia's childish affection would fade with time.

Yet now, as both had reached marrying age, their bond seemed only to deepen. If his daughter was to find a proper husband, there was only one thing left to do—secure an engagement before Peter could propose.

Still, Herr Grob assumed there was no hurry. Surely, Peter would not act without first seeking his permission.

"Amalia, I realize you are young and may not yet understand how much famine and sickness destroy lives. But your future, health and happiness, depend on choosing the right husband. A man who remains at home, and can provide, may one day mean the difference between life and death."

Her father's practical reasoning had always clashed with Amalia's passionate nature. She felt she would die if she could not be with Peter—and she refused to surrender to Herr Grob's control. She was struggling to find the right words to delay him, when a knock sounded at the door.

Herr Grob smiled with satisfaction. "That will be the pastor. I have asked him to help us select some eligible men. We can invite them to dinner one at a time, and you can decide if any suit you."

Amalia struggled to hide her dismay as the pastor entered and took a seat. He carried a list of Reformed men with good social standing—landowners or tradesmen with secure prospects.

"I assume you are prepared with a dowry, the pastor said matter-of-factly, as though he discussed such things every day."

Herr Grob nodded. "I have been saving since the day she was born."

Amalia's dowry had been quietly accumulating throughout the years. It included a set of hand painted dishes, along with embroidered wall hangings, and fine linen sheets and tablecloths that her mother had helped her stitch on winter evenings beside the fire. They were all tucked into the sturdy walnut chest her father had carved while she was still a baby. Her dowry would eventually include two milk cows, and six fine chickens along with fifty silver francs counted in the small leather pouch her father kept locked in his safebox.

In the village of Obstalden, such a dowry was generous for the times. It was enough to help a young couple begin their life on a farm. Her trousseau also held a blue wool shawl, her mother's family Bible, and a set of brass candlesticks. These latter tokens were not of wealth, but gifts of the past from Grob family members who had moved on to their eternal rest. Amalia's unspoken hope was that her husband would value her, not just for what she brought, but for who she was. And she was confident that Peter met that desire.

The men paused to study Amalia as though she were a cow on display. Struggling to maintain her composure, she smiled politely at the pastor, while inside, she wanted to scream.

Why did women have so little say about their own lives?

Herr Grob and the pastor began discussing each man's assets while Amalia sat quietly, forcing herself to listen with polite attention.

There was Herr Blumer, who owned a great deal of land inherited from his grandfather. He had been well-to-do for most of his life, and to Amalia, he seemed spoiled. She kept her opinions to herself, yet could not help but suspect that a man like Herr Blumer knew only how to count money—not earn it.

If his home and crops were ever destroyed by a foehn wind, she doubted he would know how to survive. Unlike

Peter Britt, Herr Blumer had never struggled to make a living.

Although Peter's name was not on the list, Amalia could not help but compare him to each man. She quickly realized that, by her father's standards, Peter would be unacceptable in many ways. He rarely attended church, owned no land, and often had to travel beyond the canton—even beyond Switzerland—to earn a living.

"Herr Heinrich owns an Alpenhaus and runs cows and goats up to the higher meadows," the pastor offered.

Herr Grob glanced at Amalia. "What do you think? You've become quite the mountain goat yourself."

"I am not sure I care for spending summers on the mountain," Amalia replied carefully. "I have always preferred the warmer weather in the lower elevations during those months."

Yet in truth, she knew she could endure the mountains if it meant being with the man she loved.

"Herr Rudolf is a merchant from Elm," the pastor said.

Herr Grob waved his hand dismissively. "I am not interested in anyone who travels for a living or lives too far from Obstalden."

Amalia felt a flicker of relief. Perhaps her father's objection to Peter had less to do with the man himself and more with the prospect of her being left alone—uncertain whether her husband was safe or would ever return home.

She understood his concerns. In truth, she too preferred the idea of a husband who stayed nearby. But her love for Peter had changed everything.

If she were Peter's wife, she would gladly wait for his return, as Dora did for Jakob. She could picture it already—passing the days beside Dora, gathering herbs, preparing remedies, and quietly filling the hours while awaiting the safe return of the men they loved.

The two men continued to discuss potential suitors while Amalia's thoughts drifted. She wondered how she might convince her father to approve her choice of marriage.

The two men soon agreed on the first potential suitor—a carpenter named Herr Franz. Amalia had scarcely seen him around the village, let alone spoken to him. He was at least twelve years her senior, and compared to Peter Britt's youthful face, he struck her as looking like an old goat.

She was sighing quietly when she overheard the pastor remark that Herr Franz liked blue—and detested the color red.

A tiny smile flickered at the corner of her lips. She was glad the pastor had mentioned this, for she had the perfect ribbon—a swatch of fine red silk, a gift from Peter, brought all the way from France.

Amalia was up early on Sunday morning, twisting her hair into an ornate braid. Carefully, she wove the red silk ribbon through it, securing it in such a way that it could not be removed without undoing her hair. She knew her father would never ask her to take her hair down—it would be as improper as asking a woman to undress.

During breakfast before church, Herr Grob did a double take, his gaze fixed on the red ribbon threaded throughout her braid.

"Amalia! Did you not hear the pastor say that Herr Franz despises the color red?"

She widened her eyes in feigned surprise. "But Vater, I looked out the window and saw the Glarus flag flying from the church this morning, and thought it a good day to wear red."

Herr Grob frowned. "Just because the flag is red is no reason to offend our dinner guest."

Amalia had already prepared her response and spoke quickly—perhaps too quickly. "Well, if red is going to offend him, there will be plenty of opportunities for him to be upset. We live under a red flag, with cows and people wearing all manner of red ribbons and red embroidery. Why, even the geraniums in the window boxes are red."

Herr Grob looked toward his wife. "Maria, can you talk some sense into your daughter?"

Maria set the buttermilk on the table and began ladling out the barley porridge. "She's making sense to me. Besides, there's no time for her to fix her hair now."

She glanced at Amalia and gave her a quick wink.

After a dull church service, dinner felt stiff and formal. To make matters worse, no one spoke as they ate. Maria remained quiet, as she always did in the presence of men, and Amalia refused to act friendly. Herr Grob was left to fill the silence with talk of the weather, while Herr Franz eagerly devoured Maria's tender pork roast and potatoes.

Mid-bite, Herr Franz paused to stare at Amalia's red ribbon. "Did you help prepare this fine meal?" he asked, speaking with his mouth full.

Amalia grimaced in disgust.

Before she could reply, her younger brother Fridolin—ever the clever one—spoke up in her place. "Oh no, you wouldn't want to eat anything that one cooks. She needs lessons."

Herr Grob shot his son a look that could have cracked stone, but Amalia could barely hide her amusement. She silently vowed to reward Fridolin with his favorite apple strudel—if ever they had enough flour and sugar to spare.

After that disastrous dinner, tensions only grew between Amalia and her father. Herr Grob suggested she begin helping with the meals so the next suitor could sample her cooking. After all, as a potential wife, a man would surely want to know what kind of cook he was getting.

The next dinner guest mentioned his fondness for potatoes, and Herr Grob passed this along to the women in the kitchen through Fridolin.

Amalia promptly forgot about the potato cheese bake in the oven—at least until smoke began filling the entire house.

If Maria suspected her daughter's intentions to sabotage the meal, she said nothing. Once again, the meal thwarted Herr Grob's plans to help Amalia secure a husband.

Perhaps in an attempt to catch Amalia off guard, Herr Grob began bringing men home for supper during the week. Soon there were other suitors—and more botched meals than he could count.

One evening, there was too much salt in the pastry, another, too little in the roast.

But nothing topped the evening when a chicken somehow found its way into the house, fluttered across the table, and laid an egg right next to the cream pitcher.

Amalia and Fridolin could scarcely believe the perfect timing of that prank. They struggled to keep straight faces as laughter threatened to overtake them.

During these weeks, Peter was away from the canton. Amalia could hardly wait to tell him what was happening, but she dared not write about her dining adventures. Her father might find a way to break the seal and discover proof of the game she was playing. No, she would have to wait to tell Peter in person.

One afternoon, Herr Grob burst through the door, waving a letter in his hand. "As long as you and Peter keep writing to each other, you'll never be ready for a husband. It's time for you to grow up, Amalia."

"But Vater, he's been my friend for years. Surely you don't expect me to be rude to him."

"I don't want you to be rude to him—I want you to stop writing to him."

13 Gleaners

AFTER HIS RECENT PARADE of suitors, Amalia did her utmost to avoid Herr Grob. She wished to steer clear of further conversation, lest she unwittingly betray her secret engagement. Assisting Ursula in gathering food and clothing for the poor gave her both a purpose and an excuse to stay away from the house while she awaited Peter's return to the canton.

Each morning, the young women ventured out to the farmers' fields to gather stray fruit—whatever had fallen to the earth or was deemed too bruised or spoiled to sell. Amalia was surprised by how many baskets they filled, and she was moved by her friend's generosity in sharing the bounty with those in need.

The famines of recent years had made life difficult for many, but they were especially hard on Ursula and her mother, who had so many young mouths to feed. Nothing could go to waste. Even this humble, windfallen fruit, overlooked by the reapers, might mean the difference between life and death.

The pears were picked while still green, yet even there, many were left behind due to blight and bruising. As they gathered several baskets of the hard fruit, Amalia wondered if her neighbor, Herr Kubli, was intentionally leaving extra for Ursula and her family.

As they worked, Ursula seemed unaware that many of the discarded pears looked perfectly fine. She spoke eagerly of her dream of moving to America, her words full of hope and possibility. Amalia listened with a faint smile, though her own thoughts drifted elsewhere. For Ursula, America was a promise of freedom and new beginnings. For Amalia, nothing mattered more than the quiet, aching hope that Peter would come home soon.

Ursula's voice broke through Amalia's thoughts.

"Of course, I wouldn't go until the children are older and some of them can help Mutter. But can you imagine having so much land that you can grow whatever you want? I heard they can even grow cotton and wheat."

Amalia had never imagined Ursula being anything but a wife—perhaps a shopkeeper or cheesemaker, depending on whom she married. The idea of Ursula speaking so freely about such a distant dream caught her off guard. "Ursula, do you want to be a farmer?"

"A farmer's wife would be nice. It's better than spinning like my Mutter. I don't know how she does it—sitting and spinning for days without end. It makes her back ache and her shoulders hurt, and she hardly has time for anything else. Even then, it barely puts food on the table. And I have to cook it, because she's too busy to prepare meals."

Amalia felt a twinge of guilt. Her own mother had it so much easier. But it was Ursula's talk of going to America that unsettled her most.

"What if your husband doesn't want to go to America?"

Ursula rolled her eyes. "Maybe I won't get a husband. I don't want to get married and have a brat every year like Mutter. Babies steal your life. No, I'd rather go to America alone. Or maybe I'll marry a man once I get there."

Amalia stared at her, caught between admiration and unease. Ursula's words were bolder than anything Amalia would dare to say aloud.

Trying to hide her shock, Amalia changed the subject. "I hear no one's allowed to harvest their potatoes at the community garden until they're large enough to make a meal."

Ursula picked up a basket full of pears and balanced it on her hip. "Ja, that's another way to stretch the food as far as possible. A larger potato fills the stomach faster than a smaller one."

Amalia picked up her basket and followed her friend. "Is it true there will be fines for those who harvest early? I've never heard of such a thing. What do you think?"

"It's true. They're even posting guards at the community garden to be sure no one steals what isn't theirs."

Amalia was surprised at how much her friend knew about the new potato law. "I guess I have no idea what happens at the community garden."

Ursula laughed. "You don't need to—you have a garden in your yard. Those of us with large families and little land must rely on it for food. As a matter of fact, I'm one of the guards to make sure no one steals. Each family takes a turn on night watch."

After a day of picking up and hauling baskets of pears and apples from the fields to the priest's house, Amalia was exhausted and sore. She was also sad to realize her friend had such a difficult life.

As soon as she arrived home, Herr Grob met her at the door, his expression tight with displeasure.

"There you are. I've been asking where you were, and no one seemed to know."

"I told Mutter I'd be with Ursula harvesting fruit."

"Your mother has gone to help a sick friend and didn't have time to prepare the evening meal."

Without arguing, Amalia slipped past him and set to work. She cut up bread, cheese, and dried ham, and heated milk soup to make a light supper. Her hands moved quickly, while her mind simmered. By the time her mother and Fridolin returned, the table was set and ready.

Herr Grob broke the brief peace. "I'm not sure gleaning for culls is proper work for you, *Mousekin*. Why can't you stay home and embroider or knit, like other young women?"

Amalia pressed her lips together, fighting the urge to roll her eyes. She knew better than to answer sharply. "But Vater, didn't you teach me that it's our God-given duty to help the poor?"

Herr Grob's mouth tightened. "I expect you to serve the Lord by preparing to be a good wife. That would put you in a far better position to find a husband."

Amalia said nothing more, though her stomach twisted. No matter what she did, it always came back to this, marriage, obedience, and duty. She longed to share her heart, but she knew better than to challenge him.

Amalia held her tongue, but as soon as Fridolin went to his room and her parents settled by the fire, she carried the dishes into the kitchen, drew the locket from her blouse, and gazed inside.

"Oh, Peter," she whispered, with a tight throat. "I'm not sure how much longer I can handle Vater. Please come home."

She heard footsteps behind her, and turned around to see Maria entering the kitchen, to fetch a glass of water. Her mother stopped short and stood frozen, eyes fixed on the locket in Amalia's hands.

Neither she nor her friends wore jewelry. A good Christian woman dressed simply and modestly. Zwingli himself had preached self-denial and warned against any show of riches. Such adornment was frowned upon by the pastors and elders. And now here stood her only daughter, the girl she had raised, holding such an abomination.

Amalia spun around, her voice low and urgent. "It's not what you think, Mutter. Please... don't say anything."

Maria stepped closer, her gaze unwavering. "May I see it?"

Reluctantly, Amalia handed it over. "Peter gave it to me."

Maria's fingers brushed the locket gently, her expression softening in spite of herself. "It's beautiful," she murmured, but concern lingered in her eyes. "But it must have been expensive."

Amalia's lips curved into a wistful smile. She ached to share the news of her secret engagement, but the words caught in her throat. "Peter gave it to me so I can remember him while he's gone."

Maria opened the locket and studied the tiny portrait. "I see that he makes you happy," she said quietly, her sternness fading as she handed it back.

"He does, Mutter. And if you can keep my secret, I'll show you something else."

Intrigued, Maria watched as Amalia carefully slid Peter's picture aside to reveal a hidden portrait of her mother.

Maria's eyes widened, then softened into a rare, almost shy smile. "It's a good likeness, even if I say so myself."

Amalia felt her heart ease. Somehow, this forbidden jewelry had melted her mother's reserve and warmed her heart toward Peter. If only Herr Grob were as easily swayed.

14 Barefoot

WHEN THEY WEREN'T GATHERING culls from the orchards, Ursula and Amalia went door to door collecting second-hand clothing to distribute. A few people had clothing that had been outgrown, and they were glad to contribute to helping their neighbors. But it bothered Amalia that a fair amount came from people who had passed away.

While sorting boots and shoes, Amalia paused, her fingers lingering on a pair of small, knitted boots. She let out a quiet sigh. "It seems unfair that so many babies die each winter."

"Ja, it's heartbreaking," Ursula said, though her voice held little warmth. She tossed a pair of trousers onto the heap of men's clothing without so much as a glance at the tiny boots. "But it also means one less mouth to feed—and gives the others a better chance to live."

Amalia flinched at the bluntness of her friend's words. She was struck by how easily Ursula dismissed the loss of life all around them. Then again, perhaps sorrow and suffering had left her numb, after nursing sick siblings and watching them slip away.

Amalia had a faint memory of her mother losing a sick baby when she herself was still a young child. She could hardly remember the baby's face—or even whether it had been a boy or a girl. Her mother never spoke of that child, and Amalia had never felt it was right to ask. Nearly everyone she knew had lost a sibling or child. Perhaps that was why her father was so protective of her.

She hoped the healing remedies passed down by the Britt ancestors might help prevent such losses. But even with those remedies, Dora had likely lost a few of her own, especially given the twelve-year age gap between Peter and his brother Kaspar.

Father Huber's charity workers seemed to be multiplying. Amalia noticed that many wore rags and looked as thin as the grey herons down by the Walensee. They moved quietly among one another—bound by a kinship she longed to share. She couldn't help but feel overdressed and she had never known the hollow ache of hunger that most of them had endured.

One day, it struck her that preparing a meal for potential suitors was a luxury these workers could scarcely imagine. Her face burned with shame as she realized how she'd been wasteful, ruining good food simply because she wanted to cook for the man she loved.

One morning, on her way to Father Huber's house, Amalia spotted Dora in the village. Dora rushed over, eager with good news.

"The men are home. They're with Andreas at the Alpenhaus right now."

Filled with anticipation to see her beloved, Amalia quickly sorted through the clothing, then turned to Ursula with a plea.

"Would you keep my secret while I run up the mountain to meet Peter?"

Ursula smiled and waved her on.

When she caught sight of his familiar form, Amalia ran to Peter, her heart singing as she fell into his embrace. Jakob Britt stood nearby, watching with quiet satisfaction as his son joyfully held his future bride. Peter had confided in him, but Jakob would never betray their secret.

If anyone understood what Herr Grob was capable of, it was Jakob Britt. He had long witnessed how his old friend scorned the Glarus Emigration Society and looked down upon anyone bold enough to dream of a new life in America.

The young couple sat on a log to catch up on all the things they couldn't write in letters, while Jakob turned back toward the Alpenhaus, where his wife was sure to be cooking him a delicious meal.

Amalia told Peter about working with Ursula. She thought about entertaining him with stories of the tricks she and Fridolin had devised to thwart the suitors, but with her new awareness, it no longer seemed as amusing as it once had.

"I'm glad you're back. I've been discouraged trying to put off Vater's plans."

Peter was surprised to hear of Herr Grob's insistence that Amalia be courted by other men.

"I thought he would realize we care for each other by now."

"It's not the caring—it's the trade. He's afraid for me to marry someone who can't offer a stable life."

"When I come home from the Dresden Academy, I'll be able to draw and paint anyone. He'll see what I'm capable of."

Amalia's gaze fell at the thought of waiting until Peter finished his studies before they could marry.

"Do we have to wait that long?"

Peter swept his long arm across her shoulders and gave them a reassuring squeeze.

"Stay strong, just a little longer. I have a special painting planned. Once I show him what I can do, I'll ask for his permission to marry you."

"I do think Ursula is right. Vater just needs to recognize your talent." Her eyes lit up. "What are you going to paint?"

Peter winked. "It's a surprise."

Amalia returned to the village with a song on her lips and a spring in her step. She felt confident that Peter knew what he was doing—and in no time at all, she would become Mrs. Peter Britt.

The next afternoon, Amalia followed Ursula through a small canyon on the outskirts of the village and up into the low hills. Carrying a basket of mixed fruit and a sheet filled with clothing, they crossed a creek to reach an old farmhouse.

The house was attached to a small barn, and both looked worn and weary. A cow stuck her head out as they passed, watching them with mild curiosity. They climbed the worn steps to a sagging porch that looked ready to tumble into the creek below.

It had been quite a trek. Amalia had no idea what Ursula had packed in the sheet, but it was heavy and she was grateful for a chance to catch her breath, while Ursula knocked on the door.

She expected the inhabitants to be infirm or elderly, since most villagers came down to Father Huber's house to collect what they needed.

To her surprise, the door opened and a flock of barefoot children, all under ten, poured out, moving so quickly she couldn't count them. This family was even larger than Ursula's.

They introduced themselves and the mother, barefoot like her children, gave her name as Lisbeth. When they opened the sheet, it revealed children's clothing of all sizes and two pairs of women's shoes. Amalia wished they had shoes for the children too. She could only imagine how cold their little feet were in the winter.

While the girls tried on dresses and the boys were given trousers, Lisbeth gratefully sorted the apples, setting aside those that needed to be cut and dried first. When she opened the pantry to store the unripe pears, several chickens fluttered into the living area, adding to the chaos.

Ursula held up two pairs of shoes. Amalia felt relieved when one fit Lisbeth perfectly.

"What else do you need for the winter? Do you have enough blankets?" Ursula asked.

"Ja. We could use blankets. The girls have scarves, but the boys need hats to keep their heads warm," Lisbeth replied.

Amalia couldn't take her eyes off of the children's bare feet. She'd lived her entire life surrounded by simple comforts, never realizing how others survived without the basics.

She had always owned head coverings and shoes, and there had always been plenty of blankets to keep warm. As she looked around the drafty farmhouse, she noticed two homemade straw mats laid across the plank floor. In the corner stood a rough wooden bed layered with shabby blankets and a couple of sheepskins. The thought of facing winter in such conditions made her shiver.

"What about food?" Ursula asked gently. "Do you have enough supplies?"

"We get eggs from the chickens, and the cow still has milk for now. My brother-in-law keeps us stocked with barley and cheese from the family farm, but flour would help, if anyone can spare some."

"And wood? Do you have enough for the winter?"

"Ah, yes. My husband stacked plenty before he died, and his brother has promised to help until the boys are old enough."

Amalia's heart sank. She hadn't realized Lisbeth was recently widowed—how dreadful to be left alone with so many children.

As they prepared to leave, a wisp of a girl ran up and held out her hand. In it was a rough piece of pink quartz.

Hesitant to take it, Amalia met the child's deep blue eyes and realized her refusal might do more harm than good.

"What's your name?"

"Rosa," the girl lisped, then leaned close as if sharing a secret. "Don't you wish you had a little child like me?"

For a fleeting moment, Amalia did. She longed to scoop Rosa up, slip shoes onto her feet, and wrap her in a warm coat. Instead, she accepted the gift with gratitude and hugged the child tightly.

As they crossed back over the shallow creek, Amalia couldn't stop thinking about Rosa's tiny hand and earnest eyes.

They talked quietly about where they might find wool hats and scarves for the children, then fell silent, each lost in thought.

Amalia couldn't shake the image of Rosa. Herr Grob's words echoed in her mind—about marrying a man who could provide. To him, that meant security, even survival. But even a good provider could die young. The thought of raising a flock of children alone filled her with quiet dread.

Later, as she stepped through her own door, her mother hurried to warm a bowl of soup. Herr Grob looked up from his Bible.

"Ah, Mousekin, we're glad to see you home safe."

Amalia paused. She saw a tenderness in her father's eyes that she hadn't noticed before.

15 Birnbrot

BEFORE HE FELL IN love with Amalia, Peter's two great passions in life were art and nature—an inheritance from the generations of Britts who came before him. He had grown up planting and gleaning from nature's bounty with his mother, but he'd also learned to carve wood and make portraits by mixing paint at his father's knee. His family taught him to utilize nature's resources and enjoy its art in every way, including the human form.

His desire to make art left Peter dreaming of studying at the Academy of Fine Arts in Dresden, Germany. He'd started traveling to earn money for his education, but one famine after another had thwarted his plans as he ended up helping to provide for his family instead.

While visiting Dresden, he had viewed the Old Masters Gallery, where Raphael's *Sistine Madonna* was displayed. Renaissance artist and master painter Raphael had been commissioned by the Pope to create the *Madonna* in 1512. It had remained relatively unknown for nearly 250 years—until it was brought to Dresden in the 1750s.

By the time Peter observed the *Sistine Madonna*, it was on its way to becoming a beloved icon. The larger painting had become popular in music, literature, art, and design. Many artists had copied variations of the *Madonna*, inspiring Peter to create his own version with Amalia as his subject.

The following day, Peter got up early to sort through his father's studio. He found a flax cloth and stretched it over a wooden frame before sketching it with charcoal. Next, he mixed pigments with linseed oil. He smiled as he laid the first brushstrokes onto the canvas.

Like Raphael's *Madonna*, Peter portrayed Amalia with flowing hair that merged into a flowing scarf. This head covering maintained the purity of his subject while alluding to her feminine beauty. Amalia's innocent features replaced Raphael's childlike *Madonna*. He chose to reflect the style and form of the old master while infusing more light into his version—creating what he thought of as a more radiant *Madonna*.

When it came time to paint the Christ Child, Peter was relieved to find sketches of Ursula's baby sisters in his satchel. Setting the twins' portrait on a shelf, he was pleased to see how much his skills had grown. He had no intention of painting anything too risqué—after all, this was a religious subject—but he felt it might look more realistic if the baby were pulling at the top of her dress just a little.

Smoothing lighter shades of paint across the forehead and nose brought a new thrill as he saw the emerging contours of Amalia's face. He carefully adjusted the lines with a stroke here and there until her expression and spirit seemed to shine out from the canvas.

One thing Peter didn't imitate from the *Sistine Madonna* was the angels at the bottom of the painting. By the early 1800s, those angels had taken on a life of their own. Copied into paintings and drawings, they had become popular—often minus the *Madonna*. Peter was not a religious man and he had little interest in painting otherworldly beings. The angels represented fiction to him. He wanted to make this *Madonna* his own, and he wanted nothing to distract from Amalia's beauty.

Painting his *Madonna* was a sacred experience for Peter—but not in the way some might think. Although not a Christian, he admired the innocence and purity of his precious Amalia. It was her tenderness and kindness toward little children and elderly people. It was her modesty, combined with her great beauty. She was everything he had ever desired in a woman. As he put the finishing touches on the baby, he dreamed of the day Amalia would bear him a child, because he believed she would make a wonderful mother.

After hours of painting, he stretched his stiff neck and shook out his sore arm from so many adjustments. Finally, he added a highlight to each eye. Standing back to admire his masterpiece, he was elated to see how lifelike she appeared. The child was crying, as babies often do, while

Amalia shone in all her glory as his *Madonna*. For just a moment, Peter wondered if perhaps there was a God in heaven—because someone seemed to be smiling down on him.

At the Grob house, Amalia was creating her own work of art. Birnbrot was one of Peter's favorite foods, and as she set out each ingredient, she prayed it would meet his expectations. Every baker had their own recipe, often created by many adjustments over the years. Purists preferred only pears and apples, while others experimented with plums, figs, and apricots. Most included some variation of walnuts, raisins, cinnamon, cloves, and anise.

Amalia pre-soaked the raisins until they were plump and juicy before boiling them with dried pears, apples, plums, and some orange peel. Then, she carefully drizzled honey into the flour and yeast mixture to ensure the wrap-around dough had just the right texture. Before baking, she poked holes in the outer dough and washed it with egg. Once it had baked to golden perfection, she set it aside to serve her guests with cheese and coffee.

The scent of the freshly baked birnbrot drew Fridolin and Herr Grob into the kitchen. Maria swatted them away and told them no one would eat a bite until it was served to their company.

Amalia gave her mother a grateful smile. She was eager for her engagement to stop being a secret. She knew Maria was trying to convince Herr Grob that this was a good match—possibly one made in heaven.

When she had convinced her father to invite the Britt family to the Grob home for Sunday dinner, Amalia knew she was taking a risk. She'd been ruining meals, and now she was taking care to create the perfect dinner. Herr Grob had been patient with what seemed like mistakes in his daughter's cooking, but after this meal, he'd know she could cook when she wanted to.

With tantalizing scents in the air, the Grob family rushed around the house. Maria put the finishing touches on the table setting while Amalia and Fridolin ran upstairs to put on their best clothes. Amalia whispered a prayer and pinched her cheeks before rushing downstairs—just in time to find Herr Grob welcoming the Britt family into their home.

16 Madonna

WHEN THE MAIN MEAL was finished, Maria set out the coffee, cheese, and birnbrot. While Amalia sliced the dessert, Peter unwrapped his masterpiece and propped it on an empty chair. Both families sat in silence. Nothing so grand and beautiful had ever graced the Grob home.

Amalia was so touched by the painting's luminescent beauty that she forgot to sit down and stood between the kitchen and the table, staring at it. She recognized her face, but she was struck by the beauty that Peter saw in her. She had always dreamed of being a mother, and her eyes filled with tears to see a baby in her arms. The day of Peter's secret proposal had been the happiest day of her life, and she was excited to realize her dreams were finally coming true.

Maria glowed with pride as she compared her daughter's face to the painting. "It's beautiful! And such an accurate likeness! It's obvious you have great talent."

Fridolin pointed at the image, using the nickname he had for his sister. "It's Molly." He carefully ran his fingers across the hand-carved frame surrounding the painting.

Peter smiled. "My Vater made the frame."

"Ah, but a frame is nothing without the painting." Jakob Britt's eyes shone—not because of his own fine craftsmanship, but because he was proud of his son's talent.

It was evident that everybody liked the painting—except for Herr Grob, who barely glanced at it. Finally, he spoke.

"What is this?"

"Vater! It's the mother of Jesus." Amalia's voice cracked with disappointment at her father's apparent disrespect toward Peter.

"Yes, but where do we find such paintings? Are we papists? Didn't Zwingli call such things idols? Did he bring the Reformation to Glarus three hundred years ago and die a martyr so my only daughter could be worshiped as the Catholic Madonna? I think not!"

Peter tried to defend his work. "Why does anyone have to worship it?"

Herr Grob not only refused to look at the painting, but also refused to look at Peter.

"Such a painting disgraces our family and might even affect her ability to find a proper husband."

"But I love your daughter and I would do nothing to harm her. As for her finding a husband, I hope to marry her myself—if you would give your permission, sir."

There, he said it. It wasn't how he'd planned to ask Herr Grob, but his love, as evidenced by the painting, was no longer a secret.

"You do not fit the criteria of the man I want my daughter to marry." Herr Grob's voice was gruff.

Maria set her fork down with a bang.

If Peter was angry, he didn't show it. "Tell me your criteria, sir."

"It's not possible for you—you'll never make anything of yourself. Life is about surviving, not drawing pictures and constant traveling."

"But Vater, I love him. I want to marry him." Amalia tried to choke back the tears.

"As God is my witness, I sure hope not. Peter has disavowed our beliefs, and now you've become part of it by being in that painting." He spat out the words. "I did not raise you to pose as a papal idol."

Herr Grob was angry. The Catholics and Protestants in Glarus had drawn a firm line between them, and in his opinion, Peter had crossed it.

Peter tried to explain, "But I am not a papist, nor do I plan to become one. I simply painted a picture of the Christian Madonna and child."

Herr Grob glared at Peter, his brows running together in a deep furrow while his voice thundered. "I don't care who and what you paint, but you're not marrying my daughter."

For the first time in his life, Peter felt helpless. He was used to applying his creativity to solve problems, but this time, his talent had cost him the one thing he desired most.

Humiliated and with nothing left to say, Peter stood up and walked out the door.

Dora humbly thanked Maria for dinner before following her son.

Jakob Britt stood up too, but he couldn't leave without speaking his mind.

"Don't think I can't see what's happening here, Grob. Peter is a good man who serves others and respects his elders. You're not rejecting my son because of his character or lack of love—but because you disapprove of how he makes his living. We've been friends for many years, and yet you must also disapprove of how I make my living." With those words, he left, slamming the door behind him.

So many voices speaking loud and fast had left Amalia's head spinning. When it became apparent that her worst fears had come true—that there could be no marriage without her father's permission—she burst into tears.

"What about me? Do you not care what I want, Vater?"

Herr Grob turned toward Amalia, and his eyes softened with compassion. He lowered his voice as if he were coaxing a favorite cow.

"There, there, my dear Mousekin, I know this is hard for you, but my job as a father is not to indulge your fantasies but to help you choose an industrious husband who can provide a stable home. It's better to stop this nonsense now before it gets harder."

If Amalia sensed tenderness in her father's voice, she refused to acknowledge it.

"Don't call me that. I'm not your little mouse anymore."

Without waiting to hear another word, she ran up the stairs to her room.

Whether Herr Grob recognized Peter's value or not, Amalia did. Peter could grow, paint, or build anything he set his mind to do. She knew of no other man as kind, hardworking, and talented as Peter Britt—and there was no other man she wanted to marry. Since her father disapproved of their union, everything she'd hoped and dreamed about was lost.

Maria Grob hated conflict. She hoped the men could come to an agreement because she wanted her daughter to be happy. Left to pick up the pieces, she grabbed an apple off the table and went upstairs to offer words of comfort.

Amalia stared out the window, searching for where Peter might have gone. After finding no sign of him, she turned to her mother.

"Why are we women bound to do whatever our fathers and husbands command?"

"You know, daughter, that it's a woman's duty to obey men—first our fathers, and then our husbands."

"But it doesn't seem fair that we spend our entire lives waiting for men to tell us what to do."

"It's not our place to question why. The Good Book simply tells us to submit to them."

"But why can't women choose what they want?"

"Because God himself is male, and he made men to lead us."

"So, God is like all the other controlling men? If that's the case, I don't like God very much."

Maria gasped. "Amalia! What kind of blasphemy is this? Jesus didn't teach the disciples to say, 'Our Mother who art in heaven.' Our job as women is to obey and support the men that God, in his sovereignty, has placed over us."

Amalia remained silent, staring out the window. Realizing her daughter wished to be alone, Maria went back downstairs.

The Madonna painting remained on the chair where Peter left it. The family stumbled around it for three days without speaking about it. Then, one day, it mysteriously disappeared. Whether her father gave it back to Peter or stored it somewhere in the attic, Amalia never found out, but it made her angry that such a work of love was rejected, ignored, and then disposed of—without even asking her permission.

17 Secrets

AMALIA WALKED TO URSULA'S house, scarcely noticing the burnished gold on the leaves of the pear orchard. Autumn, once her favorite season, had lost its charm. She hadn't heard from Peter all week. To fill the silence, she busied herself helping Ursula, who moved briskly from task to task—harvesting food, drying fruit, and gathering clothing for the poor. Yet no matter how busy she stayed, beneath every chore, lay the ache of what she had once dreamed would be her engagement celebration.

Sheltered by her parents and church, Amalia knew very little about the Madonna. One afternoon while they were sorting the clothing, it occurred to her that Ursula had knowledge she didn't.

"Why would anyone pray to the Madonna?"

Ursula tossed a stack of dirty shirts over her shoulder into the wash pile before she answered.

"Because Mary is the mother of Jesus."

"But doesn't it make more sense to pray to Jesus?"

"Of course we pray to Jesus, but some people find comfort in praying to the mother of Jesus just as others find comfort in praying to his father."

Amalia could understand why some people preferred to pray to a woman instead of a man. For the first time, she realized Catholics were much like herself, finite beings who were just trying to understand God.

Each day as Amalia left the house, Herr Grob didn't ask where she was going, and she didn't bother to tell him. In fact, she refused to speak to him at all. She couldn't forgive him for treating Peter with such disrespect.

She couldn't blame Peter if he chose to disappear. Still, the silence between herself and Peter gnawed like an open wound. She longed for some sign, any word, to know that he was all right. But as the days slipped by, she began to wonder if he had left the canton. She prayed he wouldn't take her father's angry words to heart, and vanish from her life forever.

After a week of anxious days, she came home, checked the stone fence, and found a feather. It was plain and gray, and she had no idea what kind of bird it came from. It could've been lying on the ground anywhere, but it was in her secret hiding place, so she knew it was from Peter. Her heart soared with relief, knowing that Peter was thinking of her—until Herr Grob's angry words echoed in her mind, reminding her once again, that it was her father's will that would decide whether they could ever be married.

Excited to know he was still in the canton, she rushed out of the house before Herr Grob got home for lunch. Knowing her mother would assume she was working with Ursula, she headed straight to the Britt farm in Obstalden.

Peter and Jacob Britt had just returned from taking a boat across the lake to Quinten, where the sun-warmed slopes yielded bushels of grapes and figs, fruits they couldn't grow in their narrow valley.

Dora, who was sorting the ripe fruit, looked up and greeted her with a warm smile. Relief washed over Amalia, mingling with gratitude. Despite Herr Grob's harsh words, nothing had changed between them. Peter's family welcomed her in the same friendly way they always had, as if she was a member of the family.

Peter led Amalia outside where they could speak in private. She took a seat on the bench while he paced in front of her. His footsteps were quick and restless and he seemed more anxious than on the day he proposed. Amalia couldn't help but wonder what was troubling him now. Surely, by this point, he was used to her father's disapproval.

He sighed. "Ah, my darling, being together might be more difficult than we thought, but I still believe it's possible."

At the affectionate term, she could feel her cheeks growing warm again.

"What do you mean?"

"Well, we can't marry here in the canton without your father's permission, but I've thought of a way we could be together, if you're willing."

Amalia drew in a deep breath, wondering what he was about to say. Peter did the same, hoping she wouldn't be shocked by his words.

"My Vater and Bruder have been thinking about emigrating to America. If we join them, we can get married once we leave."

The trees, with their gold and red leaves, suddenly began to spin around her. Surely he wasn't serious. Relief filled her to know that Peter still wanted to marry her, but emigrating had never crossed her mind. It was something women like Ursula thought about, women without a man.

It seemed a cruel twist of fate that she could have the man she wanted, yet couldn't be with him, unless she left everything, and everyone she'd ever known. Her emotions rushed to the surface, panic rising in her throat.

"But I'll never see my family again."

Peter listened carefully, before he replied.

"Or we might persuade them to come with us."

She shook her head.

"Vater would never leave Switzerland. He's angry at yours for speaking about it. He calls it nonsense."

"But is it nonsense? We'd have more farming opportunities without the foehn winds, and we'd be free to marry in America."

He stared so intently into her eyes that, for a moment, she felt like jumping on a ship and leaving immediately.

"But what about your education? Couldn't we just move to Dresden? At least then, we'd still be on the same continent."

This time, Peter shook his head.

"What good is an art degree, if I can't make a living here in the canton? And what good is being on the same continent, if your father is so angry he won't even speak to us? America offers both the freedom and opportunities we need."

"When is your family leaving? If I don't go, will you leave without me?"

Her lip trembled as she spoke. She felt a doomed sense of loss, as if they had already gone without her.

"My dear Amalia, surely you know the last thing I want to do is leave without you."

Her face grew warm again, this time with shame. Of course he didn't want to leave without her. That was the whole point of the feather—to remind her he was still here, planning for their future.

"I do want to marry you. It's just—I've never thought about leaving Switzerland. I've never even left the canton."

Peter gently placed his finger on her lip.

"Shhh, don't say any more right now. Nothing is decided yet. I only want to know how you feel. Don't answer until you've had time to think it through. This isn't the sort of decision to rush."

At his touch, she melted and her racing heart slowed. Soothed by the softness in his voice and the steady warmth of his gaze, she realized he was right. This was too big to decide in a moment of fear or longing. Emigrating would mean more than simply becoming his wife—it would mean leaving behind everything she'd ever known.

"Kaspar and his wife are coming up the mountain for a meeting tomorrow to discuss their plans. Would you like to join us?"

"I'll tell Mutter I'm helping a sick family and come up the mountain when Vater leaves for work."

Amalia walked much slower on her way home, she was surprised by how easy it had become to deceive her father. It had all started with one small sin of omission—keeping her engagement a secret. This had led to her pretending she couldn't cook, just to discourage suitors. Now she was seeing Peter behind her father's back. Keeping a secret was one thing. Wearing forbidden jewelry was another. Wasting food felt shameful enough—but leaving without saying goodbye to her family felt like the worst kind of betrayal.

Amalia wasn't sure she could do it—and yet she couldn't imagine her life without Peter. Either choice left her sick with dread.

Once she arrived home, the Grob family sat down to another quiet supper. Herr Grob, tired of his daughter's silence, turned to his wife.

"Is Amalia unwell?"

"Why don't you ask her yourself? She's sitting at the table with us."

Silence resumed until Fridolin began slurping his soup noisily. When no one reacted, he belched loudly. Maria, who usually scolded her son for poor manners, continued eating in silence. Fridolin glanced around the table for a response, but his parents and sister kept eating with glum faces, as quietly as possible.

Amalia looked around at their beloved faces. The thought of never sitting at this table again softened her feelings toward each of them.

She caught a glimpse of compassion in her mother's eyes. How could she ever leave without hugging her goodbye?

Fridolin, annoying as he could be, was still a good brother. The thought of not watching him grow up filled her with sorrow.

Her father, despite everything, had always treasured her and only wanted the best for her. The idea of betraying him again broke her heart, and she had to blink rapidly to hold back the tears.

Why couldn't he understand her love for Peter? Didn't he see he was forcing her to choose—between the man she loved and the family she couldn't bear to leave?

18 Fears

When Amalia arrived at the Alpenhaus the following day, Peter's brother Kaspar and his wife Anna had already arrived with their children.

Dora set a pot of coffee on the table while Jakob pulled out a chair for Amalia. "Welcome to our family meeting." His fatherly smile was comforting.

From the other room, a feeble voice called out, "Jakob? Is that you?"

Jakob rose and went to the doorway. "Yes, Onkel Andreas, we're all here. How are you today?"

"Oh, I'm about as lazy as that cat that couldn't keep the mice out of the barn."

Jakob chuckled. "You remember that cat, Onkel? We're having a family meeting. We're discussing the possibility of going to America—what do you think?"

"We used to have plenty of food to go around. I'm not sure why these damn foehn winds keep destroying the harvests these last few years, but if America doesn't have foehn winds, I say leave and don't look back. If I were young, I'd go with you."

"Your wisdom will be noted at the table."

"I wish you well, nephew. I'm going to take a nap."

With that, the older man drifted off to sleep, and Jakob shut the door to keep the noise out of his room.

Jakob turned to those sitting around the table. "Who wants to share their thoughts about going to America?"

Anna glanced toward Kaspar. "I think it sounds like a lot of hard work, maybe more than we know."

Kaspar seemed more optimistic. "I like the freedom it offers. I'm interested in becoming a pastor. I want to live where I don't have to worry about offending the local government or the church. Most importantly, I hope to find enough land to farm and make a living to support my family."

Amalia studied Kaspar's face while he spoke. She marveled at how much he looked like Peter—strong jaw, high forehead—but not the same eyes. Something about the twinkle in Peter's eyes made her feel like she could do anything. Still, Kaspar had joined the Reformed faith and was now a devout Christian, so she asked him the question on her mind.

"Do you believe it's God's will for us to emigrate to America? My Vater says we are predestined to live here. He says we were born Swiss, which alone is proof of where God wants us. He believes emigrating defies God's sovereign will."

Kaspar shut his eyes for a second as if he were going to pray. "I don't want to speak for God, but to be honest with you, I'm not convinced God's will is manifested by the things that happen to us. Perhaps it's God's will for us to make our own choices."

Jakob turned to Amalia. "How do you feel?"

"My biggest concern is the people I'd be leaving behind. I can't imagine never seeing my family again."

The corner of Anna's mouth twisted as she nodded to Amalia with empathy. "I can't blame anyone who doesn't want to go. There's so much we'd be leaving behind—friends, family, a childhood home full of memories, our beautiful mountains..." Her voice trailed off as if she were about to cry.

Amalia was relieved to hear another woman express her fears. It was good to know she wasn't alone.

Dora stirred some cream into her coffee. "The thought of getting on a ship terrifies me. I hear that many people get sick, and some even die before they reach land. And there's also the chance of a shipwreck. I feel a bit like Herr Grob—if God wanted us to travel by ship, why didn't he give us fins like a fish?"

Peter chuckled. "Mutter, you wouldn't have your delicious grapes right now if Vater and I had not stepped on a boat to get them."

Dora grinned at her youngest son as though she felt silly. It was apparent they loved each other. Amalia wondered why her father couldn't take her disagreements with him in such a pleasant manner.

Jakob looked tenderly at his wife. "It is a lot to ask, but we must also consider how terrible the crops have been these last few years. Our only choice might be to leave or starve."

Peter met Amalia's eyes as he spoke. "There are many reasons for leaving, but only one is essential for me—I want to marry the woman I love. And, of course, that depends on whether Amalia is willing to go with me."

Amalia smiled lovingly at him and tried to ignore the sinking feeling in her stomach. She was beginning to realize the sacrifices she'd need to make to become Peter's wife.

Kaspar changed the subject to discuss how they could raise the funds. "I hear the people traveling with the Glarus Immigration Society will have their entire way paid, plus free land when they arrive."

The lines on Jakob's forehead deepened with concern. "That might be true, but they'll also be obligated to remain in one place and give up a portion of their crops until their debt has been paid."

"Would that be so bad, Vater? After struggling with the farm, paying fares for a wife and children seems steep and hard to come by." Kaspar's face was starting to show the same lines as his father's.

Jakob shook his head. "If we go, we can't be beholden to anyone."

Peter nodded. "We'll have more freedom if we pay our own fares." Ever the wanderer, the thought of staying in one town didn't seem feasible to him.

Kaspar shook his head. "In that case, we'll also need to save money to buy land."

Dora, who managed the garden, let out a low sigh. "Our potato harvest is poor this year. We won't have any to sell—we'll be lucky to feed the family."

Jakob had pulled out his knife and whittled on a small stick as he listened to each person share their concerns. "Peter and I can travel to earn money if the rest of you can make our supplies last another winter."

"What port would we leave from? Will we go to New York?" Kaspar seemed eager to leave as soon as possible.

Amalia was surprised to see Peter sit up straight as if he were about to give a lecture. "The shortest route is to leave from Le Havre, France. Their ports have been rebuilt since Napoleon's day. It's one of the fastest routes to America. It sails directly to New Orleans, Louisiana. They also speak French there, so we should find it easy to communicate."

Jakob slapped his younger son on the back. "Good plan. I've always said your travels have been a good education."

Dora wiped up some milk that one of the children had spilled. "How long will it take to reach the ship?"

Peter reached for a slate tablet to estimate the time it would take.

"We can take a barge down the Linth to Zurich. From there, we can take a riverboat to Basel, and we can take a carriage across France until we reach the coast. It will take about twenty-four days."

Amalia gasped as softly as possible. They would travel nearly a month just to reach the ship. This journey was more than she had ever imagined taking in her lifetime. How could Peter ask this of her? Why did her father demand that she obey him and find a different husband? Why did she have no say about her future?

They spent the rest of the afternoon discussing what it would be like to live in America.

Dora hoped to grow figs. Peter wanted his own vineyard. Kaspar wondered if the cattle would be easier to manage on flat ground. Jakob, still whittling, said he couldn't wait to open his own furniture shop.

In the middle of their musing, Amalia asked what the weather would be like.

Jakob shook his head. "Every time a letter comes from America, the writer describes a different type of weather—some say it's hot without snow, while others have described deep snowdrifts with a long winter. I guess we'll just have to see when we get there."

Anna's eyes grew round and wide as she spoke. "A cousin of my mother's wrote to us about a terrible wind that wasn't hot like these foehn winds, but it came out of nowhere and did a terrible amount of damage. It tore their entire house apart."

Their chatter gave way to silence as the weight of uncertainty settled over them. The foehn winds brought threats to the Glarner people that no one could control. The type of storms they might encounter in the new world wasn't a consideration to take lightly.

When it came time for her to head home, Peter walked Amalia down the mountain, holding her hand.

"How do you feel about America?"

"Honestly? I'm frightened, but I want to be with you."

"What concerns you the most?"

"All of it—leaving my family, the possibility of getting sick at sea, surviving storms, and even being shipwrecked. And that's before arriving in the new land, where we'll need to speak a new language, eat strange foods, deal with the weather—just to start our lives over."

Peter nodded. "It is a lot to think about, but you still have plenty of time. You don't have to decide yet. It'll probably take me at least a year to raise the funds."

Amalia wasn't sure if that was good or bad. The idea of waiting a year for him to raise the money—and taking such a long trip before even getting on the ship—was daunting. Her father would surely attempt to have her married off by then.

"If I go to America, Vater will be furious, and Mutter will cry."

"I understand how painful that will be, but I hope you can decide what is best for you."

"Here in the canton, I need Vater's permission to marry, but leaving unmarried will shame my reputation and fami-ly."

"There are ways to save your honor. We could marry on the ship and write a letter when we arrive."

"Will your Bruder be able to afford taking Anna and the children with him?"

"My Vater and I might need to help him, but don't wor-ry—I'll make sure your fare is covered."

Peter's willingness to take such measures to include her in his life encouraged Amalia to pursue their dream of marrying, starting a family, and building a home—even if it was on a different continent. Still, she shuddered at the thought of such a long trip.

When they stopped in Herr Kubli's pear orchard, she lingered in Peter's warm embrace before continuing on to the Grob house alone.

The candles had already been lit in the windows. She paused to look at the only home she'd ever known, memorizing each plank, window box, and shutter. She hoped the memory of it would never fade. The smoke from the chimney beckoned, revealing the warmth inside. And even when the fire went out, it remained a cozy home with warm duvets, plenty of candles and lanterns, and enough food to fill her belly. She'd be trading all these comforts for who knows what—possibly a rough cabin in the wilderness without any guarantee that she would survive.

She'd been fortunate to have a father who provided for her. With his stability, she'd enjoyed homemaking pursuits like baking and embroidery, while other girls her age had been forced to work in the factories. She valued Herr Grob's capacity for maintaining things as they were, but she also admired Peter's ability to change with the seasons. She wondered which method was better—to stay the same or to change. Due to the famines and foehn winds, it might only be a matter of time before Herr Grob himself needed to find new ways to survive.

When she got home after supper, her family assumed she was late because she was helping Ursula, as she hoped they would. Her mother rushed to get her something to eat, but

Herr Grob cleared his throat as though he had something important to say.

"Amalia, did we not discuss how you were to focus on homemaking tasks to prepare for being a wife, instead of all this charity work? What will it take for you to obey my request?"

Already bone tired and weary from trying to sort out her life—a dilemma created by a father who only saw things his way and showed little concern for her feelings, she was in no mood to talk.

"I don't know, Vater. I have a terrible headache and need to lie down."

Without waiting for her mother to bring food, she went straight upstairs to her room.

As she climbed the steps, she remembered how Peter had once jumped into the Walensee to retrieve an empty wooden box that had fallen overboard from a merchant's boat. After the rescue, he'd tied a string of empty boxes together to pull them across the water behind the boat. This left room for more goods inside the small craft. The grateful peddler had thanked him profusely, then said, "You can always trust Peter Britt to think of a new way to do things."

The old peddler had spoken the truth. No one was more resourceful than Peter.

Amalia would need versatile thinking, perhaps stepping outside the canton, even beyond her faith and family, if she were to become his wife.

19 Rosa

Even though Amalia adored Peter and couldn't imagine life without him, she began waking each morning with a pounding headache from sleepless nights or a sour stomach from the stress of her decision. At times, she wished someone else would choose for her—just to escape the crushing weight of its consequences.

One noontime, just as the Grob family was sitting down to eat, Ursula knocked on the door. "Lisbeth has a sick child who's struggling to breathe. Her son ran down to ask Father Huber to pray—but I thought you might have a potion that could help."

Amalia grabbed her rucksack and shawl and rushed out the door without waiting for permission. Her parents had heard the conversation. Her mother would only worry about her catching something, and with a child's life at stake, there was no time to argue with Herr Grob about helping the sick.

As they hiked up into the hills, both young women began to cough as they passed through a thick cloud of smoke.

"The farmers must be burning their fields." Amalia stopped to pull her scarf over her nose and mouth. Like most Glarner women, she wore it draped over her dress—but it proved especially useful at times like this.

Ursula hurried ahead, leading the way. "I doubt it's time for the burning—the root vegetables still need to be harvested before the frost." She paused to tighten her own scarf across her face before adding, "Father Huber says a lightning strike started a fire in the next valley, and the smoke is drifting this way."

Amalia coughed again. "That might explain why this child is having trouble breathing." She made a mental note to check the herbs in her rucksack. Hopefully, she'd brought the essentials.

Since she'd begun helping Dora, Amalia had seen more death than she cared to remember. It wasn't as hard when someone had lived a long life, but it was heartbreaking to watch babies and children succumb to the diseases that kept sweeping through the canton. She wondered if children in America died as easily as Swiss children.

"We can't save them all," Dora had once said gently. "Every winter, more children die than we can help—but when one pulls through, it means everything to that child and their parents."

They marched on through the thick smoke, Ursula chattering about village gossip, while Amalia drifted into her own thoughts. She barely heard a word because her mind was so knotted with conflicting feelings. She didn't mean to ignore her friend, but she could think of little else besides the possibility of leaving her family, her home, and the country she loved to follow Peter. Why must life be filled with such difficult choices?

As they crossed the creek and entered the yard, the smoke thickened until they could barely make out the shapes of the house and barn. The air stung their eyes and clung to their throats as an older girl opened the door and silently ushered them inside. The warmth of the hearth offered little comfort against the choking haze.

A small form was curled on a cot near the fire.

Amalia's heart dropped—it was Rosa. Her tiny frame looked even smaller in the dim light, her breathing shallow and raspy. Too weak to speak, she met Amalia's gaze with wide, frightened eyes. Something inside Amalia tightened. She reached for the child's hand and made herself a silent promise—this one was going to live.

Amalia remembered Dora's advice. "Let the steam chase the cough from their lungs."

She asked Ursula to boil some water, then sorted through her rucksack, pulling out horehound, licorice root, and chamomile. She wished she had hyssop and thyme, but her collection wasn't as complete as Dora's.

Once the water was ready, she poured a cup and draped a towel over Rosa's head, urging her to breathe in the steam. Then she directed Ursula to make a syrup with the herbs and honey. Amalia prayed one of the remedies would ease the child's congestion.

If she could just steady Rosa's breathing long enough to get some syrup down, it might help—but progress was slow.

Amalia had never prayed so hard as she did that afternoon. The other children sensed their sister was in danger and grew very quiet. The only sounds in the house were the ticking of the kitchen clock and the raspy struggle of little Rosa's breathing.

After several hours of steam treatments, the tiny girl finally began to breathe more easily. At last, Amalia was able to give her some cough syrup. Though Rosa still wheezed, by bedtime her breathing had steadied. Hope returned to the house, and the other children began to talk and play softly.

When Ursula left, Amalia noticed the dark circles under the mother's eyes. Her heart ached for the young widow. "Go ahead and rest. I'll stay with her and call you if she gets worse."

The exhausted mother stumbled to the bed in the corner and soon fell asleep. One by one, the other children snuggled in beside her. Even Rosa gave a sleepy smile as she looked up at Amalia, as though she were an angel sent to help her.

Sitting alone with her thoughts, Amalia reflected on how quickly Lisbeth's life had changed. One moment, she had a husband to share the load—and the next, a terrible accident had taken him from the family. Caring for children was hard enough when they were healthy, but it must feel unbearable when they were sick. Amalia shuddered to think what might happen if the others came down with whatever was ailing Rosa.

She recalled Herr Grob's advice to marry a man who stayed close to home. She'd been angry when he said it—but this was what life looked like with no man around for months at a time. As much as she hated to admit it, her father was right. A husband who travels and is rarely home makes for a lonely life—almost as desolate as widowhood.

But Peter was right too. Life was uncertain—either of them could be taken by accident or illness at any time—which made the time they had together all the more precious.

Going to America offered a better chance—not just for his ability to make a living, but for their future. A chance to build something new, together.

She'd promised Peter an answer, and now she finally had it.

Looking down at Rosa, sleeping peacefully for the first time all day, Amalia felt a quiet resolve settle over her. She would go—not just for Peter, but for herself. For the life she longed to build, and the love she couldn't bear to lose.

20 Blood Moon

WHEN AMALIA WOKE ON a cot beside Rosa, it was afternoon. She was relieved to see the little girl joyfully playing with a homemade doll. The toy was no longer than her forearm and stitched together from stained scraps of linen, its seams worn and frayed. Though it had no face, a mop of yarn crowned its head, which tilted to one side, as if it, too, were weary from a long, sleepless night spent caring for a sick child.

Rosa's siblings appeared well, and glad to see Amalia wake up, so they could play noisily again. Amalia admired Lisbeth's ability to manage her family, which was probably essential for a single mother of so many children.

It was late afternoon when Amalia left the little farmhouse full of children behind and crossed the creek. The main thought on her mind was to find Peter and let him know that she was willing to follow him to America. She'd sent word home with Ursula the night before, that she'd be staying throughout the night and she decided the best way to escape her father's scrutiny was to let him believe she remained at Lisbeth's, tending to sick children.

She thought it best to avoid the village altogether by hiking through the hills. It would take longer, but she felt sure she could reach the Alpenhaus well before dusk.

The air was still quite thick with smoke. As she passed other mountain farms along the way, she could barely see the buildings. As she climbed higher, she was relieved to see the smoke thinning out, but the air still carried the sharp, acrid scent of burning wood, and each breath left a sting in her throat.

As she approached the Alpenhaus, it was nearly dark, but its outline was clearer than any of the buildings she'd passed along the way.

She called out hello, as the old wooden steps creaked beneath her feet, and Peter opened the door with a smile. She stooped to enter the room, to find him alone with Onkel Andreas.

"Vater and Mutter went to Glarus Town, this may be the last chance to shop in the city before the snows arrive."

Peter sat down to the table, a lantern casting a soft, flickering glow over the pages of his sketchbook. Sensing he was in the middle of something, she waited with anticipation as she stepped behind him and leaned gently over his shoulder, her fingertips gently brushing the fabric of his shirt.

"What are you drawing?"

Peter leaned into her touch but kept his eyes on the page. Only when he had finished, did he close the sketchbook with a soft thud and turn to face her.

"I'm making a record of the weather," he glanced toward Onkel Andreas who nodded. "We always keep track so we can plan for future years."

Amalia was puzzled. "But if you're going to America, how will a record of Glarus weather help?"

Peter sighed. "We aren't sure when we'll leave, we could be here another year. And there's still a chance we might not go at all."

Amalia's heart sunk. Now that she was finally committed, the possibility of staying hadn't crossed her mind. The uncertainty of it all unsettled her. She drew her shawl tighter around her shoulders and turned away to cough.

"My throat is so dry. It must be the smoke."

"It's bothering everyone!" Onkel Andreas cleared his own throat as he spoke. "A farmer on the other side of the mountains told Jacob it's even worse over there! There must be a fire somewhere, and the smoke is blowing our way."

Amalia walked over to the sideboard to fetch a drink, but the pitcher was empty, so she stepped outside to fill it at the well.

The pasture near the barn was usually a tranquil scene, but one glance outside made Amalia's breath catch in her throat. Rising through the smoky haze, the full moon glowed a deep, blood red.

Nothing could have prepared her for such a vision. She shuddered. There was only one thing she feared more than fire, and that was God's judgment. The thought of standing before God, found wanting, had haunted her since childhood. And now, here she was, with Peter, against her father's will. She could hear Herr Grob's stern voice in her mind as clearly as if he stood beside her.

"The moon shall be turned into blood before the great and terrible day of the Lord comes."

She didn't need to go home to hear him read it, she'd heard it so often she knew it by heart. But what did it mean? Was this a sign? Would there be an earthquake? Would the sun refuse to shine? What fate awaited her if the end truly was near?

A wave of terror gripped her. She'd brought this upon herself by lying, sneaking about, and choosing Peter over obedience. Her hand trembling, she clutched the empty pitcher to her chest, and stumbled back into the cabin with terror etched across her face.

Alarmed by her expression, Peter rose at once and reached for her, but she pulled away.

"Look!" She pointed toward the window.

He stooped to look out the tiny pane. "Ah. The moon has turned red!" His voice sounded joyful and his face was filled with awe. His response was the opposite of her rising panic and left her feeling alone.

"But I've heard the pastor preach," she whispered. "About that great and terrible day of the Lord. What if this is it?"

Peter opened the door to get a better look, but slammed it shut when a gust of smoke blew into his face, making him cough.

"I'm not sure all those Bible prophecies apply to every situation," he turned back to her. "They were written centuries ago. How do we know which words are meant for this moment?" His eyes met hers with compassion. "I don't believe this is a divine punishment, it's more likely just nature taking its course."

"But Vater would say it's a judgment from God." Her voice broke as she sank into a chair and buried her face in her hands.

Peter sat down beside her, listening as she poured out her fears. When she was finished, he spoke softly.

"I still think there must be some natural explanation."

From the other side of the room, Onkel Andreas finally stopped coughing long enough to add his thoughts. "I saw a blood moon once when I was a boy, it happened long ago, and it surely wasn't the end of the world!"

Amalia lifted her head with hope. "Are you sure? It frightens me to even look at it."

The old man smiled gently. "Perhaps because you were taught to fear it."

Peter reached for her hand, but Amalia pulled it back.

"Come on, my love, why don't we walk down to the river and see if the moon is reflected on the water? I might even paint it." He looked into her eyes tenderly. "It's not the first red moon, and I doubt it will be the last."

Amalia had no desire to see that eerie red glow mirrored across the surface of the Walensee, but if she was willing to follow Peter to America this was a small step. She wrapped her shawl across her shoulders and pulled her scarf over her face as she followed Peter out the door.

Refusing to look at the sky, she kept her eyes fixed on the rocks scattered across the trail, while her hand clung to the warmth of Peter's hand over hers.

They walked in silence, their footsteps crunching softly on the rocky path as they wound their way down the mountain and toward the river. The lower they went, the more the smoke hung in the air like a mist, muting the sights of the village.

Somewhere in the distance, a cow lowed and a dog barked, but the world seemed hushed, as if everything and everyone was watching the sky in anticipation of a terrible event.

As soon as they reached the bluff overlooking the river, Peter spoke.

"Look! Isn't it beautiful?"

Reluctantly, Amalia lifted her eyes and followed his gaze. The Valensee rippled in the moonlight. Across its surface, glowed a red ribbon, as the moon's shape was blurred by the water's gentle movement. The red looked softer there, less threatening, and almost beautiful.

Peter drew her close with his arm. "Isn't it strange how something that frightens us can also be beautiful, depending on how we look at it?"

Amalia leaned her head on his shoulder until a cough tore at her throat, and she pulled her scarf higher over her nose.

Peter glanced at her. "Whatever this is, whether it's fog, smoke, harvest moon, it's all part of nature, just as our lives are, everything comes and goes at nature's command."

Amalia still felt uncertain. "But what if it's more than that?" Her voice was shaky. "What if it's a sign?"

Peter looked back at the water, before turning to her with a smile. "Then let it be a sign that we're still alive, and walking beneath the same moon. That we still have choices."

His words comforted her like a warm cup of tea, not hot, but just enough to keep the chill at bay.

Amalia glanced down at their joined hands, then back at the water, where the moon's reflection still taunted her.

"I suppose even signs can be misunderstood!"

Peter winked. "Especially by those who are afraid!"

They stood in silence for a while, listening to the wind move through the grass and the gentle lap of water at the shore as a boat passed far below them.

Then they continued along the trail and climbed to a rocky overlook high above the lake. Peter paused again, his gaze fixed on the vista below, then he began to describe how to capture the scene in a painting, how the haze blurred the edges, how the ribbon of fire danced across the waves.

Amalia listened, trying to focus on his words, but as his description stretched into minutes, her heart began to beat faster and faster with anticipation. She'd been waiting for the right moment and finally, she could no longer hold back her news. Her voice broke into his words with breathless joy.

"I'm going with you!"

Peter turned back to her and immediately wrapped his warm arms around her in a tight embrace.

Despite the blood moon hanging over their heads, Amalia had never felt so safe.

21 Potatoes

THE FULL MOON, THOUGH tinged with red, gave enough light that they scarcely needed the lantern Peter carried, until they stepped deeper into the forest on their way back toward the village.

Peter wrapped his hand over Amalia's. "My darling, you've made me a happy man! The moon will soon be white again, and before we can count three hundred nights, we'll be on our way to our new life in America!"

Amalia squeezed his hand. "Three hundred nights? I don't think I can wait that long to be your wife!"

"I'll need to earn enough for our fares and some money to set up a studio. It might take a few months, perhaps a year."

She nudged his shoulder playfully. "That's a long time to be in France. What if you forget about me, and fall in love with some beautiful Fräulein in Paris?"

He chuckled. "Then I shall keep you well informed, by drawing her portrait in a letter, and sending it to you."

They laughed at the absurdity of Peter announcing such a betrayal through the post.

His voice grew serious again. "I'll need to leave as soon as this smoke clears."

For a moment, Amalia felt the weight of his decision, as if he were already gone.

"I don't want you to go. I'd be happy if you were never out of my sight again!"

"Well, if that's truly your wish, then you must allow me to leave just once more, so I can earn our passage. After that, we'll be together always."

He stopped walking and drew her close. "Wait, we're almost back to the village, and I want to kiss you!"

Perhaps it was the ominous red moon hanging over her shoulder. Or the thought of some mysterious Fräulein in France stealing her beloved. Or maybe it was the joyful thought of them finally being together, never more to part. But Amalia kissed Peter like she'd never kissed him before.

They clung to each other for a few seconds, both wishing this moment would never end. As they resumed their walk in silence, each was consumed with their own thoughts.

Neither noticed that they were passing the community gardens, until someone leapt from the bushes, banging on a cowbell, while another thrust a lantern into their faces.

Startled by the sudden noise, Amalia froze in place.

A voice shouted, "We've got someone over here!"

Peter tightened his grip on Amalia's hand and tried to walk on, but another voice commanded, "Stop! You must wait for the authorities!"

Struggling to make sense of it, Amalia suddenly recognized the high-pitched voice.

"Ursula!" And then it hit her. The potato guards!

"It's me, Ursula!" she called out. "I don't want your potatoes!"

But it was too late. Ursula had already raised a horn to her lips and was blowing a loud blast, while her companion ran across the field shouting for the police. One by one, lanterns flared to life as startled villagers emerged from their houses, drawn by the ruckus.

Before they could explain, the guards shoved Peter and Amalia into a nearby house, where a small crowd had already gathered to await the authorities.

The lawman stormed in, shouting before the door had even been closed.

"Search their pockets!"

The guards complied, but found nothing except for the bundle of herbs in Amalia's rucksack, which she'd carried for the sick children.

Despite no evidence, the officer launched into a full interrogation.

"What are your names?"

"Where did you come from?"

"Why are you out at this late hour?"

The questions came so fast and furious that Amalia barely had a chance to answer them before another voice cut through the noise.

"Daughter, did you steal any potatoes?"

She turned to find Herr Grob standing in the doorway, his face grim and unreadable.

She shook her head. "Of course not, Vater! I'd never dream of it!"

"Then what were you doing near the gardens so late at night?"

The room fell into silence. The villagers, most of them fond of kind, dutiful Amalia, seemed to hold their collective breath. None of them could picture her as a thief, but still, they waited for her answer.

Amalia lowered her eyes. To admit she'd been with Peter would provoke her father's wrath, likely more than if she'd been stealing potatoes. He might forgive a person driven by hunger. But a disobedient daughter, sneaking off with a man behind his back? There was no greater shame.

With the memory of the blood-red moon still vivid in her mind and the fear of divine judgment heavy on her heart, Amalia took a deep breath.

"I was with Peter."

The room fell silent. Some women turned away out of respect, to avert their eyes from her shame. Others stared with thinly veiled glee, clearly satisfied that she'd been caught. But no glance, full of pity or scorn, could compare to her father's disappointed face.

Herr Grob's face turned as red as the moon. Then, without looking at her, he turned to the officer.

"Sir, I know for a fact my daughter is telling the truth. Until tonight, she's never been the type to sneak about and lie."

Amalia's cheeks burned as she stared at her father's boots, struggling to hold her composure. His words weren't loud, but they landed like a blow.

Seeing Herr Grob's rising color and clenched jaw, the officer misread his anger, believing it was on behalf of a wrongly accused daughter. He raised his voice to the crowd.

"No one stole any potatoes tonight. Everybody can go back to bed."

Amalia reached for Peter's hand, but Herr Grob stepped between them, seizing her arm and pulling her firmly to his side. Turning to Peter, his voice was low and threatening,

"I forbid you to speak to my daughter ever again."

Amalia saw grief flash across Peter's face, but there was nothing she could do. Head bowed, she turned away, and followed her father in silence, focusing on each step as they walked through the village, then up the steps into the house.

Once inside, her hands trembled as Herr Grob turned to face her.

"I spoke the truth tonight, Amalia, but I saved my disappointment for this private moment." His voice was tight with restrained fury. "I cannot believe you've been seeing that useless vagabond behind my back. I forbid you to speak to him ever again."

With that, he took the lantern and disappeared into his room, leaving her to stumble up the stairs in darkness.

In her bedroom, Amalia stripped off her dress and collapsed onto the bed. Too ashamed to let anyone hear her cry, she buried her face in the pillow, smothering her sobs.

She had already lost her father's respect.

Must she lose Peter too?

22 Silence

THE SUN WAS WELL over the Alps by the time Amalia finally fell into a troubled sleep. When she awoke, her mother was preparing the midday meal. A strong wind had swept through the valley during the night, carrying away much of the smoke that had choked the sky.

Herr Grob came home for lunch, but they ate in silence. He made no mention of the night before and avoided eye contact with Amalia, disappearing soon after to oversee his building project.

Maria looked tenderly at her daughter's red, swollen eyes. After hearing her husband's side of the story, she knew there was little she could do to persuade him once he'd made up his mind, but she tried to comfort Amalia with reassuring words.

"Be patient, daughter, and wait on God's will."

"How can I know God's will when Vater's will is the only one that matters in this house?"

Maria shrugged. "Regardless of your father's opinion, he can't stop Peter from loving you any more than he can stop you from loving Peter. In time, you will discern God's will."

Amalia bit her lip, gathered the plates, and carried them to the kitchen. "I hope you're right."

For a moment, Amalia almost confided in Maria about her plans to go to America. But she hesitated—unsure if her mother could keep such a secret. The news would devastate her, and Herr Grob would notice the change in her mood. He'd ask questions, and Maria, gentle as she was, might not be able to hide the truth. It wouldn't take much for her to reveal everything—and then he would try to stop them.

So instead, Amalia washed the dishes in silence.

Despite her father's threat for Peter to leave her alone, she didn't think Peter would obey him. He was most likely already working to earn the money for their passage. It was up to her to wait patiently, just as her mother had said.

But patience proved harder than Amalia had expected.

The next day passed without a word from Peter. Or the next. By the third day, her heart was twisting with worry. Had her father gone to see Peter again? Had he threatened him with something worse?

Each morning after Herr Grob went to work, she slipped outside to the rock wall and slid her hand behind the loose stone where they had once exchanged secret notes. But the space was always empty. Each night, before going to bed, she checked the fence again. Nothing.

Just as Peter and Onkel Andreas had suspected, the red moon soon vanished, and life carried on as usual—at least for everyone else. But not for Amalia. For her, time stood still.

Shame crept in as she replayed her fears, realizing that night might have been the last moment she'd share with Peter for a long time. Her heart ached every time she remembered how they had parted—with no embrace, no tender words, not even a plan to meet again.

She felt an urgent need to reconnect—to know that he was safe, that their dreams still held. Each night, she tossed and turned, whispering desperate prayers for a way to see him again. And every morning, she woke with a fragile hope, telling herself each day that she would hear from Peter, and everything would be all right.

A week went by, and then two, while Amalia continued to check the fence for a drawing, a rock, or a flower—but the secret spot remained empty.

In the past, when Peter couldn't slip a note into the fence because he was out of town, he always sent her letters from his travels. Now, she grieved that she had no way to send a letter to him. Just in case something had gotten lost on its way to her house, she began visiting the postmaster's home each day. After a week of this, the postmaster began slowly shaking his head the moment she stepped through the door.

Her heart sank with growing dread—she had no idea where Peter was, or what he might be thinking.

One morning, after yet another futile search at the fence, a painful realization settled in: Peter must have left the canton. She pulled her scarf tighter around her neck. The wind had grown colder, biting at her face, and her stomach hurt at the thought that he might not return until spring.

One morning, when Ursula knocked on the door, Maria answered and told her that Amalia was not well.

Later that day, Ursula returned with a jar of soup and a small bundle of dried herbs and flowers. But Amalia refused to see her. When Maria left the bundle on the table, Amalia picked it up and tossed it onto the compost pile.

Then she paused.

Among the crumpled stems, she spotted a familiar white bloom—a starflower. She reached in and gently pulled it free. She couldn't bring herself to waste its healing properties.

Perhaps she'd make some tea with it. Her stomach still ached every time she remembered the night of the red moon.

She also saw no one from the Britt family. It felt strange—almost unreal—that the people she had nearly called family for years had gone so silent. Their absence didn't just confuse her—it deepened her pain.

Her mind kept replaying the conversations they'd shared at the Alpenhaus about going to America. A pang of guilt rose in her chest as she recalled the moment Peter had offered to pay for her passage. At the time, she hadn't fully grasped the weight of that gift—or the depth of his devotion.

She had hesitated back then, torn between Peter and her parents, uncertain which world she truly belonged to. But now, under her father's control, her heart had only grown more certain.

She just hoped Peter knew—somehow—that her commitment to him would not waver. It had only grown stronger.

One evening at supper, Herr Grob spoke to Amalia with what appeared to be a father's loving concern.

"Throughout history, women have lost men—some to accidents, some to illness, and rarely, some to other women. And yet, they've found a way to press on. In time, many even regain their zest for living. I don't doubt that you will too. I just hope you manage it before it ruins your health."

Amalia looked up, anger flashing in her eyes. "What would you have me do, Vater?"

Herr Grob paused, then busied himself shuffling the potatoes on his plate. "Perhaps you could start by getting to know other men. You still have time to build a family and a home of your own. I've invited my cousin Karl over for Sunday dinner—and I expect you to cook for him."

Amalia's mind searched for something to say, to put this off. "But Vater, what if he's not compatible with me?"

Herr Grob didn't look up. "Perhaps if you apply yourself with the same diligence you once showed Peter, you'll be pleasantly surprised at the outcome."

Amalia opened her lips to reply. She wanted to tell him she could never love anyone the way she loved Peter. She wanted to speak of their dreams, of going to America, building a life together, and starting a family. But she shut her mouth when she remembered it wouldn't matter. A daughter and grandchildren in America would mean nothing to him. He despised the Glarus Immigration Society, saw their influence as dangerous. If she spoke, he'd only blame them for filling her head with foolish notions.

Disgusted, Amalia rose from the table and excused herself.

She saw no reason to go to bed early, because she knew sleep would not come.

From her room, Amalia could hear her parents arguing downstairs. A flicker of hope sparked within her as she caught her mother's voice rising—insisting she had no interest in cooking dinner for yet another suitor.

Amalia went to the window, as she had a thousand times before, and searched the fading landscape for any sign of Peter. Where confidence had once filled her heart, doubts loomed like storm clouds on the horizon. What would she do if Peter never reached out again—or worse, returned with another woman on his arm?

Weary of Herr Grob's schemes, and more weary still from the waiting, she stumbled to her bed, collapsed fully dressed, and buried her face in the pillow. Her sobs soaked the linen until sleep mercifully overtook her.

But as the darkness drew her in, one question clung to her thoughts—

What if Peter had already given up?

23 Cousins

ALTHOUGH KARL WAS A distant relative, Herr Grob believed he would make an adequate husband for his daughter. Like Herr Grob, he was a carpenter, and despite the famine, both men seemed to have plenty of work.

Even if this attempt failed, Herr Grob was certain that Amalia's beauty and cooking would eventually win her a good Christian man. But the truth was, Amalia had no interest in finding another. She had discovered what she wanted years ago—and no man but Peter could ever fill that role.

If it weren't for her father's ridiculous rules, she would already be a happily married woman.

Her disinterest in marrying Karl meant Amalia didn't care what he thought. When he complimented her roast, she wrinkled her nose and said she hated cooking. When he asked how many children she wanted, she replied that no one could control such things but God—so why bother guessing?

Herr Grob's eyebrows drew together at the sound of his daughter's growing ill manners, but he said nothing.

Sensing she wasn't interested in talking in front of her parents, Karl asked if she'd go for a walk with him, and Amalia agreed because she had no excuse not to.

Herr Grob's face lit with hope as they stepped out the door.

They had barely stepped off the porch when Karl spoke.

"What do you think about going to America?"

Amalia tried to hide a wry smile. She'd hate for Karl to think she was laughing at him, but it gave her a sense of satisfaction to realize that even the man her father chose was no better in this regard than the one he'd rejected.

She tossed her head with amusement and said, "My Vater despises the Glarus Emigration Society."

Karl seemed kind enough. She wished she could tell him the truth—that she was already promised and had no intentions of going to America with anyone but Peter Britt. But she feared her words would find their way back to her father.

Karl looked thoughtful. "Well, my cousin has already gone, and he promised to write and tell the rest of the Grob family what America is like. I'm not sure I'll go, but I thought it only fair to mention it, in case we were to get married, you should know that it's a possibility."

"In case you decide to put up with my cooking?" She gave him a small wink.

Karl smiled. "If you don't like to cook, and you'll become my wife, I'm willing to hire a cook."

This time Amalia laughed out loud. "That would be a ridiculous waste of money—especially in these times!"

Still, she couldn't help but admire Karl's honesty. Away from her father, he seemed less formal and almost interesting.

While Karl's plans did nothing to help Amalia fall in love with him, they amused her enough to humor him with more walks. Knowing her father's opposition to American dreamers, she began to feel sorry for Karl and even began to cook his favorite foods when he came over.

Herr Grob seemed elated with the progress of their growing friendship.

"What you had with Peter was young love. Young love can afford to be frivolous, but mature love is practical and responsible. You'll find that you'll have a different kind of love than you had with Peter—but it will grow stronger in time."

Karl was father-approved, a good provider who wanted a family. The best part was, she wouldn't have to choose between him and her parents. At least for the moment. They would likely stay in the canton, unless Karl changed his mind about America. But he hadn't mentioned it again, so she assumed he was content in the village where they had both grown up.

Despite Karl's assets and regardless of her father's optimism, Amalia was never confused. She didn't love Karl and couldn't feel any attraction to him because Peter was always on her mind.

Her days felt dark and dreary. If only she had some word from Peter, she could keep up this charade knowing their separation wouldn't last forever.

One day, Amalia ran into Peter's sister-in-law, Anna at the market. She looked pregnant again and her face radiated with joy to see her.

"Amalia, have you heard from Peter?"

"Not since the blood moon." Her face betrayed her pain. She had never hidden her love for Peter in front of his family, and she couldn't start now.

"He's been traveling with Jakob. He sent his mother a letter. I guess he's finding plenty of work."

Amalia's heart drank in every detail. What a relief to know that Peter was healthy and alive—but then a wave of disappointment washed over her. There was a time she'd received a letter from him every week.

Why had he stopped writing?

Surely, he could have sent a message to his family, who could have passed it on to her. Was he afraid of her father? Or had he given up on her?

After her conversation with Anna, Amalia felt strange. It was a different kind of pain than she had known before—a dull ache of doubt. She began to wonder if Peter still loved her, or if he had ever truly loved her at all.

She remembered how tenderly he had kissed her on the night of the blood moon—how certain she'd been of his love back then.

Why couldn't she feel it anymore?

One Sunday afternoon, Amalia was carrying the dinner plates to the kitchen when there was a knock at the front door. Karl hadn't joined them that week, and she felt a sense of relief.

Assuming it was someone for her father, she ignored the knock and let her mother answer it. But she was startled by the sound of Herr Grob yelling at someone. Curious, she stepped back into the room to find Dora Britt standing there.

24 Coffee

DORA STOOD AWKWARDLY BY the door while Herr Grob sat finishing his dessert.

He shook his head. "Come on, Dora, do you take me for a fool? I know your son will continue to pursue my daughter against my wishes. How dare you suggest she come near him under the guise of nursing the sick!" He paused to wipe his mouth with a napkin.

Dora held her head low. "And surely you know that I will be honest with you. You have offended my son and my husband, but I have no one else to help me."

"Where are the men in your family?"

"They are in Germany and will be gone all winter," Dora spoke calmly, yet firm.

"Then why can't you care for the old man yourself?"

"It's hard work hauling wood and water at the Alpenhaus, and it's easier if more than one person can share the burden of caring for the infirm. Besides, I'm often summoned to help with the sick, and someone needs to stay with my Onkel."

"Why can't you bring him down to the village?"

"He's lived his entire life up there—and that's where he wants to die."

"Well, you've come to the wrong house if you want my help. What about your daughter-in-law?"

"Kaspar's wife, Anna, is heavy with child—and she can't lug her children up the mountain."

Irritated by the interruption to his dessert, Herr Grob took a sip of coffee to wash down a bite of apple strudel, then choked when he realized Maria had switched him back to the barley coffee.

"Maria, what is this? I thought you bought coffee. Are we out again so soon?"

"No, but we must stretch what we have, or we won't have enough to last the winter."

Dora Britt saw her opportunity.

"My husband and son bring back flour, sugar, and coffee with every trip. We have a good store set aside for the winter—if you allow your daughter to stay with Andreas, I will provide you with coffee for as long as my supply lasts."

Herr Grob thought for a moment with a sour expression on his face, as though neither the barley coffee nor her suggestion were palatable.

"This is nothing more than extortion, but I suppose that's what a man has to do to get good coffee in these times."

Amalia held her breath and tried to keep a glum façade while her father bargained with Peter's mother.

"How long must she stay with you?"

"As long as Andreas needs nursing. He could die next week—or next summer."

"Next summer?!" Herr Grob barked. "I will not be giving my daughter on a permanent loan. She needs to be home by the time the cows go up the mountain."

Everyone in the room knew he really meant before Peter returns to the village in the late spring.

Herr Grob glanced at Amalia. He pondered the possibility of Peter coming back to the village, but he assumed by her long face that Peter was nowhere to be found.

"I guess you've helped us in the past, so I suppose it's only fair to loan my daughter. But adding some flour and sugar in with the coffee would definitely sweeten the deal."

As much as Amalia resented being bargained like a piece of property and spoken of as though she wasn't in the room, everyone seemed happy with the deal. Dora gained her helper, Maria was delighted to have extra flour and sugar, Herr Grob got his coffee. But Amalia got the best deal of all—a break from entertaining Karl, and an escape from Herr Grob's ever-watchful eye.

She ran up the stairs to gather her belongings. Wanting something to help pass the time while she nursed the old man, she grabbed the rag doll from the chair by her bed. She hadn't touched it since she was eight—except to dust it off occasionally—but it needed repair. There were tears in the dress, and the threads that made up one eye had partially unraveled, giving it the appearance of a permanent wink.

Perhaps she could fix it and give it to a child of her own someday.

She tossed the doll into her rucksack, raced back down the stairs, and slipped out the door before Herr Grob could change his mind.

As she hurried to catch up with Dora, she realized that not even strong black coffee could soften her father's attitude toward Peter.

25 Christmas

As Amalia followed Dora up the mountain, she began to breathe freely. It was almost like someone had been sitting on her chest, and now she was suddenly taking in air and exhaling all at once. She hadn't realized how stifling it was to live under her father's roof. She always felt his scrutinizing eye, while she pretended to enjoy Karl's company.

If she were honest, she might admit that Karl was the best of her father's chosen suitors. But it was her adoration for Peter that made him seem so mediocre.

Even his dreams of going to America were vague and ill-informed. He had no clue what route to take, and she didn't dare tell him that the best route was through Havre, France, to New Orleans and it could take twenty-four days. If Amalia said such a thing, Karl would wonder how she knew this, and it would open what Onkel Andreas called a nest of trouble.

Dora didn't say much on the way up the mountain. Amalia wondered if trading her winter's supply of so-called luxuries for Amalia's presence would create a hardship for her dear friend that she hoped would someday be her mother-in-law. She honestly doubted that her nursing skills were equal to the price of coffee and sugar. There must be another reason Dora wanted her.

As they crested the last rise and walked past the now-familiar pasture, pond, and barn, Amalia's heart ached at the sight of the Alpenhaus. For seven years, this little cabin had been her home away from home, and yet, without Peter it lost some of its charm. She thought back to the night of the blood moon, and realized how naive she was. She'd rushed up the mountain that day with so much hope in her heart, eager to tell Peter she'd go with him. Then the shock of the blood moon, mixed with her father's fearful scriptures, had stolen her joy. If only she could have foreseen how the events of that night would separate her from the man she loved. For a moment she thought she might be sick as she remembered how pained his face looked as her father forced her to follow him and walk away from Peter.

Amalia took a long look at the timeworn, weathered cabin where her love for Peter had grown. She admired its timbers, the tiny window, and even the low doorway. She ran her fingers over the lintel before stooping to go inside. It felt as though she were stepping into another world, one that Herr Grob and Karl had never entered, and never would. She felt more certain than ever that this was the world, and the family, she'd been destined for all along.

Dora broke into her thoughts. If you'll put some water on for tea, I'll check on Onkel Andreas.

Amalia set about building up the fire, boiling some water, then steeping the herbs Dora had set out. In no time, Dora emerged from the bedroom with soiled linen, which she took outside. After washing her hands, she sat down to drink a cup of tea.

It was a peaceful day. Dora gave instructions on how to care for Onkel Andreas, including how to prepare a soft soup he could eat, how to help him sit up, and how to place a pillow behind his back so he wouldn't choke while being fed. She showed her how to help him use the chamber pot and clean him afterward.

Then came the laundry, how to wash it, and hang it outside when the weather was mild, or how to pull a rope across the timbers and secure it indoors when the weather turned harsh.

Throughout the day, Dora never mentioned Peter once. Amalia silently hoped for some small anecdote or story from his travels. But Dora was practical above all, and perhaps she didn't wish to give Herr Grob any excuse to call Amalia home. Perhaps she thought the less said about her son, the better.

Dora carried a small basket of vegetables and cheese from the cellar. Together they made a simple stew for supper. It was much plainer than what Amalia was used to eating. She longed for some bread to dip into the stew, until she caught herself. Her family would be enjoying the luxuries Dora had sacrificed to have her there, and she must never let on that she wished for more.

That night, as she lay on the feather tick next to Dora, she remembered Alpabzug and how full of excitement she'd been to sleep there. She recalled listening to the Britt men yodel as they gathered the cows. Life had seemed so happy then. It had only been a couple months, yet so much had happened in such a short time. Despite all the changes, she cherished the memory of the day Peter asked her to be his wife.

She turned her face away from Dora, not wanting the older woman to see her tears. As she drifted off to sleep, she gently cradled her locket beneath her nightdress, wondering if she'd ever dare show it to Dora.

When they woke the next morning, Dora asked if she felt up to taking care of Onkel Andreas by herself. Dora needed to make good on her promise to take the supplies down to Herr Grob in exchange for Amalia's presence. They agreed that Amalia would be fine alone even if for a few days, if Dora was called to tend the sick. The cabin held plenty of wood and food, and Amalia would be safe inside if a storm came.

Amalia felt a twinge of guilt as she watched Dora adjust the heavy burlap sack on her back. The bulk of the coffee, flour, and sugar pressed the coarse fibers onto the small woman's shoulders, probably scratching through her shawl. Dora reached for one last item before stepping out the door. It was her rucksack of herbs.

As Amalia watched Dora heading down the mountain with that heavy load to satisfy Herr Grob's greed, she resolved to work hard, so Dora wouldn't regret the bargain she'd made.

Once Dora was gone, Amalia looked around the small cabin and thought of all the memories Peter and his family must have made in this place, where their family had been farming for generations. Even with their creativity and industrious mindset, for an entire family to pick up stakes and move, they must believe something was missing.

She'd always thought of them as having plenty, but now, without anyone around, she realized they were poor by Herr Grob's standards. Her father might never dream of going to America, but his life was comfortable compared to the Britts. He had no reason to leave. She marveled that despite the lack of money, the Britts seemed so much richer in laughter and love than her own family.

Dora returned that evening with something better than coffee—a letter from her husband.

It was just a simple note. A single page folded over with a seal on the outside, letting her know they'd made it to France, found some work, and would soon be sending money home.

It might not look like much on paper. No flowery declarations of love, but in a world of uncertainty, where women often wondered if their men were still alive, such a letter meant everything!

Once again, Amalia was reminded that this was why they must go to America, so the family wouldn't have to be separated.

Amalia wished the men could come home for Christmas, but considering how far they'd traveled, she knew that wasn't likely. Coming home was as much a luxury as the goods the Britt men carried home on their backs. Luxuries twice bought through hard work and sacrifice.

Just before Christmas, diphtheria hit the village. Babies were falling sick, and many of them were dying. Dora left to nurse the sick, while Amalia stayed behind to care for Onkel Andreas. Andreas seemed confused much of the time. Dora had mentioned his tremors and forgetfulness, but Amalia wasn't prepared for how much he had changed. He acted like a little child, arguing with Dora one minute, then cheerfully singing a song the next. Now it was up to Amalia to keep him content. This was a challenge, especially on the days when he forgot who she was and insisted that he was going out to round up the cattle.

He wasn't as strong as he had been just a few months earlier, so he couldn't act on his plans, but his distress at not being able to work was intense. Amalia discovered she could soothe him by singing to him.

After days alone with Onkel Andreas, Amalia thought she might lose her mind too.

She was surprised when Dora came through the door one afternoon and told her the weather was still mild, and she should go down to visit her family for Christmas. If she hurried, she might make it in time for church on Christmas Eve.

When Amalia stepped into the church, with carols ringing in her ears and heart, she never thought she'd be so happy to see Herr Grob, but her heart was warm. The physical distance between them had given her a renewed compassion for her father. Despite their differences, he'd always provided and cared for her. She didn't regret loving Peter, but she was sad that she had grieved her father.

Maria was ecstatic to see her daughter. Fridolin acted annoyed that she was back and stealing their parents' attention, but she noticed that even he was glad to see her, whether he admitted it or not. It was moments like this that filled Amalia's mind with doubts about going to America. If only Peter were with her, so she could stay grounded in their plans.

During her visit, no one mentioned Peter. Herr Grob seemed certain he was still gone from the canton, partly because of Amalia's mild manners and her willingness to interact with Karl, whom he'd invited for Christmas dinner. Karl brought a tree with him. Fridolin decorated it with pinecones, while Amalia tied red ribbons in the branches.

As in other years, her father gave her a beautiful piece of fabric she could use to make a dress. This time, it was a piece of blue silk. She held it up to her face, and her mother said it would look beautiful on her.

While visiting her parents, it was nice to enjoy a feast with luxuries like coffee, bread, strudel, and birnbrot once again.

As she watched Herr Grob relish his coffee, Amalia was glad that her hard work was able to provide it for him. But she felt a little sad when she realized she hadn't seen Dora drink coffee once since she'd been staying at the

Alpenhaus. She decided to make up for it by taking some bread and birnbrot up the mountain for Dora when she left.

26 Hunger

WINTER CAME WITH BRUTAL force that year. Winds howled down the mountains, threatening to rip away anything not anchored. Snow packed tightly around the houses, turning walking paths into tunnels. It was a bleak season—made even bleaker by Peter's absence. And when the river froze over in mid-January, it sealed off any hope of seeing him until the thaw.

The famine had already taken its toll. The closer it came to spring, the less people had to eat. Children went to bed hungry, while their mothers tried to stretch the dwindling stores. Though few starved outright, the constant hunger left them vulnerable to every wave of sickness that passed through the canton. Weakened by poor nutrition, many fell ill and Dora was often called away to care for the suffering.

The Alpenhaus cellar still contained adequate stores of cheese, dried meat, and root vegetables—along with a few apples and dried fruit. On the days when Amalia grew weary of eating the same stew again and again, she reminded herself she was one of the fortunate ones—because her belly was full.

The villagers were hungry for food, but Amalia's hunger was of a different kind. No food could fill the gnawing ache in her gut, but Peter. How she longed to see him, if only for a moment to look into his eyes, and tell him that she still loved him.

Dora rarely spoke about her son, though letters often came from Jakob, with a brief note from Peter tucked inside, sending his regards to Amalia. Though she longed to know more, Amalia had been careful not to overstep, unsure whether Dora considered her history with Peter a delicate subject best left unspoken. One morning, as Dora prepared another letter for her husband, Amalia gathered her courage.

"Would it be all right if I added a note for Peter?" she asked softly.

Dora's eyes crinkled into a smile as she handed Amalia the sheet of paper, along with the quill she'd just set down.

Amalia's fingers trembled slightly as she dipped the tip into the inkwell. The scent of the iron-rich ink tickled her nose as she carefully pressed the quill to the page. Her words flowed in looping strokes, each one infused with hope and longing. For the first time in weeks, their dreams felt tangible—as though her love could sail across the mountains and into Peter's waiting arms.

One afternoon, Amalia was spooning soup into Onkel Andreas' mouth, when he pushed the spoon away, signaling that he wanted to talk.

"Sometimes I think of Regina," he said, his voice soft with memory. "And even though it's been many years since I saw her, I still miss her."

Amalia set the bowl aside and gave him her full attention.

"I asked her to marry me, you know," he paused for a moment as though he wanted to remember every detail, some too private to share with her. Then he continued. "She wanted to be with me. We had plans—until her father put a stop to them."

"What happened?" Amalia asked, her heart beating in sympathy.

"Well, you know that a woman can't marry without her father's permission—and he wouldn't give it. So neither of us married. We still saw each other at church, at social gatherings, but we could never be alone. It was a hard burden to bear. I blame the sorrow of it on her death. One day, she just fell ill—and was gone overnight."

"You never found anyone else?"

"No," he slowly shook his head. "How could I? She was the one I loved—and I couldn't even be there to comfort her when she died."

His voice cracked for a moment as though the pain had never left him—it had simply settled quietly into the lines of his face, waiting for someone to listen.

"Do you wish you'd done anything different?" she asked gently.

"If I had the chance again," he said, his voice rough with regret, "I wouldn't have cared whether we were married. I would've declared my love openly. I would've taken her in my arms, right there in front of the whole village, and not cared what anyone thought. I would've waited for her father to die—if that's what it took—so we could marry, even if we had to wait until we were old and gray."

Amalia had always assumed Onkel Andreas remained unmarried because he was a solitary man, but now she understood—he hadn't chosen to live his life alone. It had been forced upon him. Dora's family wasn't just company to him—they were all he had.

She began to feel a deep kinship with the old man—an unspoken bond forged by dreams denied and love restrained. Few people could understand her pain, but Onkel Andreas had lived a lifetime of grief.

Despite Dora's concern that he might not survive every time she left him, Onkel Andreas clung to life. After he shared his story of lost love, Amalia found it easier than ever to care for him—her empathy deepened by the struggles they shared.

One day in early March, the sun broke through the winter gloom, casting a golden light across the mountains. The air was warm and the waterfalls were making their music. Amalia knew it was just a trick of nature—a false spring, tempting the weary Glarners to believe in warmer days ahead. She realized how fickle the weather could be, but she might as well enjoy the sunshine while it lasted. She dragged a chair outside onto the porch where she could enjoy the fresh air and a little sun on her face.

With her hands wrapped around a mug of tea, her face turned toward the sky. She drank in the fragile promise of spring—and, as always, found her thoughts drifting to Peter. Dora had mentioned it was his birthday, but Amalia didn't need the reminder. After nearly a decade of friendship, she knew this date by heart.

They'd been running low on lamp oil, so Dora had gone down to the village for supplies. A traveler passing through had warned them that typhoid was once again spreading throughout the valley. Not knowing when she might return, Dora packed her rucksack with potions and herbs and headed down the mountain.

Left alone with Onkel Andreas, Amalia's greatest fear wasn't illness—it was the threat of a Foehn wind. These sudden, warm gusts could roar down the mountainside without warning, melting snow, loosening avalanches, and drying up the water supply that farmers depended on for summer. To be fair, any wind made her uneasy—but it was the warm ones she feared most. They could arrive like a whisper and leave behind disaster.

After Dora left, Amalia rummaged through the cellar and decided to make a loaf of birnbrot in honor of Peter—even though he wasn't there to share it. There were no raisins, but she made do with what she had. As the fruit simmered and the scent filled the kitchen, she shaped the dough with care, pretending for a moment that she was already Peter's wife, living with him in the new world.

She knew so little about America—just vague notions and secondhand stories—but her mind painted their future with optimism. A land of fresh beginnings. A place where love could bloom without fear or permission. In that imagined world, she poured her heart into the birnbrot, determined to be the kind of wife Peter would be proud of.

Her thoughts turned to Ursula. For all the times she'd spoken about going to America, Amalia was still surprised that Ursula was actually planning on going alone. Amalia could scarcely summon the courage to go with Peter, let alone embark on such a journey by herself. But Ursula was different. She was bold, certain, and unshakably clear about what she wanted from life. At the thought of her friend, Amalia felt a stab of regret. She had blamed Ursula for what happened that night, but if she were honest, she knew Ursula would never try to hurt her.

Amalia couldn't bring herself to reach out and ask for forgiveness. Not yet. It didn't feel safe to confide in anyone, not even Ursula. So she held her secrets close, guarding her fragile hope of leaving with Peter until the time was right.

Dora had been gone a few hours when Amalia felt the start of a headache. At first she thought it was just eye strain from bending over her needlework in the dark cabin. The embroidery her mother had given her at Christmas was very detailed. It could also be the fact of Peter's birthday and not being able to see him, pressing on her spirit. By the time the birnbrot was baked, the dull ache had sharpened into a pounding throb behind her eyes and she sensed the weather was changing.

She pulled back the curtain and saw the sky was growing dark even though it was far too early for nightfall. The dark clouds troubled her. She couldn't yet tell if the storm carried a warm or cold wind. If it was a Foehn wind, the dry air could spark a forest fire. If it was a cold front, it might drop a foot of snow. Storms in the Alps were notoriously unpredictable.

Opening the door to test the air, she ignored a leaf that blew in as a shiver ran through her body. For the moment it seemed to be a cold wind. The sun had vanished. The wind was picking up, and thick snowflakes were beginning to fall.

When Amalia mentioned the sudden change of weather to Onkel Andreas, he just nodded and said, "It's March. The weather can never make up its mind this time of year. But don't worry—I've placed plenty of rocks on the shingles, so they won't blow away."

It was an old Glarner tradition to weigh down the shingles on the roof with stones, especially in places where the mountain winds could rip off a loose shingle in seconds.

Amalia was used to snow—she'd never known a winter without it—but it was the wind that always unnerved her. Wind, she felt, could never be trusted. As the wind began to whistle around the Alpenhaus, shrieking through the eaves and rattling the shutters, her anxiety increased. By the sound of it, the shingles might be under threat.

Panic rose in her throat.

What if the wind tore the roof off?

What if trees fell and Dora couldn't return for days?

What if old Onkel Andreas died while the storm raged outside?

Then what?

She was beginning to wish she'd never left home. Never been traded for coffee to catch a reprieve from Herr Grob's control. As her mind filled with all sorts of terrible scenarios, she was startled by a voice shouting,

"Make sure you bring in as much wood as you can before the storm hits."

It was Onkel Andreas calling from the other room. After living his entire life in this cabin, he seemed unconcerned about the wind. Despite being infirm and mostly bedridden, he was still full of wisdom. If she stayed calm and listened, he was telling her what to do.

"No matter how bad the storm, we are always safe at the back of the cabin, in the cellar if nowhere else."

She tried to imagine sleeping among the carrots, apples, and potatoes, next to a wall of cheese, but his words failed to give her comfort. Especially since the fireplace, their only source of heat, was at the front of the cabin.

"I'll feel so much better when the wind dies down," she said.

"Don't worry! I've placed heavy rocks on the shingles so they won't blow away!"

He was prone to repeat himself several times a day. She just hoped he was telling the truth.

"What if we run out of water?"

"Melt the snow!"

The old man sounded optimistic, but Amalia had to remind herself how childlike he'd become. His reassurances, though well-meaning, gave her little confidence in her own ability to take care of them throughout a storm.

As the storm grew louder, Amalia's unease deepened. The shingles might be covered with rocks, but now she questioned whether even rocks could withstand such a gale. She knew Dora would probably stay in town at this rate, but she couldn't resist looking out the window one more time.

That's when she saw a lone figure trudging through the blowing snow, heading straight for the Alpenhaus. At first, it was too far away to be certain. It could even be a mirage. Straining her eyes, she tried to make out the figure as it came closer, then her breath caught. Was she imagining things?

When she recognized the familiar satchel, a quickening stirred in her chest.

She forgot about the rocks. Forgot about the storm. And even forgot about Andreas's steeping tea.

She threw the door wide open with a joyful shout.

It was Peter.

27 Sanctuary

Peter hurried up the porch steps, dropped his satchel just inside the door, and disappeared around the side of the cabin. Moments later, he returned with an armload of wood and tossed it inside, then ran back for more. He didn't pause to greet her. His breath came in short gasps from the climb, but he moved with intention, filling the room until it looked more like a woodshed than a living area. Amalia watched in silence with a grateful heart. She realized he was preparing for the worst, making sure they'd stay warm and safe, no matter how long the storm lasted.

After latching the door and securing the shutter, he turned to her and wrapped his arms around her. They embraced in silence. Even after his breathing slowed, Amalia could feel his heart beating against her ear. Finally, they pulled back to look at each other, their eyes speaking without words.

Amalia spoke first. "I thought about you all day. I even made birnbrot. I dared to hope you might come home for your birthday, but I knew it wasn't very likely."

"Did my mother not tell you that we were coming home? My parents are staying in the village, but I had to see you."

Amalia shook her head. Maybe that's why Dora had reminded her of Peter's birthday. Surely she knew Peter might show up when she left that morning. Perhaps Dora supported their plans to marry after all.

"I met Mutter on her way down. When we saw the clouds coming over the mountain, I told her we couldn't leave you alone in such weather, so I raced the storm."

Amalia thought about the legend of the starflower. "Do you like to take risks?"

Peter laughed. "No, I hate taking risks, but I'll do whatever it takes to protect those I love."

A flush warmed her cheeks. He still loved her, despite all her father had done to drive him away.

She looked at him, eyes shining. "I only wish Vater realized what a brave man you are."

The wind rose with a roar, shaking the shutters until they clattered against the window frame. Amalia jumped as a sharp thud struck the door.

Peter glanced toward the sound and offered a reassuring smile. "Just branches," he said gently. "The wind's tossing around anything that isn't tied down."

From the back room came a drowsy voice. "Who's there?"

Peter leaned into the bedroom doorway. "It's only the storm, Onkel Andreas—but I'm here."

A soft chuckle followed. "Don't you worry. I've got plenty of rocks on the roof. They should keep the shingles in place."

As daylight slipped into night, the wind continued with wild abandon, shifting everything not anchored to the earth. The rocks on the roof seemed to be holding their place, despite the storm's fury.

Amalia was relieved to find the ache in her head fading. The sight of Peter, safe and near and still loving her, wrapped around her like a warm blanket. Even though the wind howled on, a quiet peace settled over her heart.

Peter told about a recent trip to France, recounting a portrait commission that had tested both his patience and skill. "I had a very old woman who wanted me to paint her as she looked in her youth," he said with a grin. "I told her I wasn't a miracle worker."

Amalia laughed. "What did you do?"

"I painted her face as best I could—without the lines. She seemed pleased enough."

Their laughter echoed around the room, light and cheerful against the fury of the storm, then they melted into each other's arms once more, their joy filling the room with warmth.

"When do we leave for America?"

Peter placed another log on the fire, the flames crackling as he paused to gather his thoughts.

"Amalia, there's something I need to tell you."

His tone was so serious that she held her breath, heart fluttering as she waited.

"I still need to travel—to earn more before we can go."

Her heart sank. She had hoped he was home for good, that they might leave as soon as the river thawed.

Peter looked away and bit his lip. "My brother still needs to raise more money to bring his family over. Vater and I are helping him."

Amalia nodded with understanding. The famine had left many empty-handed. Some barely had enough to survive the winter—let alone afford passage to a new world.

"I'll be going back to my Vater's house soon," Amalia said quietly. "Is there a way we can write—without him knowing? I need to hear from you. I need to know you're safe."

Peter reached for her hand. "I've missed your words too. Every day. But I was afraid to send anything to your house—it felt too risky."

Peter's stomach rumbled.

Amalia smiled. "Would you like some birnbrot and cheese?"

His eyes lit up. "You have birnbrot?" The excitement in his voice made her laugh.

She gently placed a finger to his lips. "Shhh—don't wake Andreas," she whispered. "I knew it was your birthday, and even though I didn't expect to see you, I made some—just in case."

Before she could rise to prepare the food, he pulled her into his arms and kissed her—long and hard. He was a man of few words, and she understood this was his way of saying, thank you.

While Amalia sliced the birnbrot and cheese, Peter tip-toed past the sleeping Andreas and disappeared into the cellar. Moments later, he returned with a bottle of wine cradled in his hands.

"This," he said with a grin, "will be the perfect companion to your birnbrot."

The sheepskin rug in front of the stone hearth looked inviting enough, but Peter rummaged through the old armoire and pulled out two pillows, then dragged one of the feather ticks across the wooden floor.

Amalia gathered the food and a stoneware cup. Together, they settled onto the makeshift bed by the fire, the warmth curling around them as they shared their simple feast.

Even though their dreams had to wait a little longer, they savored this delicious moment—just the two of them, alone except for the sleeping old man in the next room. The thought of one day being free to marry and begin a new life in America filled them with a giddy kind of hope. It almost seemed too good to be true, yet they had heard the stories—of Glarner families who had crossed the ocean and found land, freedom, and opportunity stretching farther than the eye could see.

The fire was warm, and the wine made Amalia drowsy. Wrapped in Peter's arms, she almost forgot the storm still raging outside. Part of her still clung to duty—still felt the pull to obey her father. She had spent a lifetime trying to earn his approval, and she knew Herr Grob would be furious if he knew she was here, alone with Peter. Yet this stormy birthday reunion felt like something worth celebrating. And who wouldn't long for loving arms on a night like this?

She laid her head on Peter's chest. "It's a dream come true—just to be with you."

He rested his cheek against her hair. "When we get to America, we'll make a lot of dreams come true."

"Will we have a pear orchard—so I can make birnbrot?"

"Of course. And peaches and apples too. And I'll open a studio and paint portraits. People will come from miles around to have their likeness captured."

He gently pulled on one of her braids, then began to untie it. "And someday, we'll have a son and a daughter. A son like me—and a daughter like you."

"But only one at a time, please." She laughed softly.

Peter kissed the top of her head. "A boy who loves to paint and grow things, and a daughter who bakes and maybe sings. Don't you think such children would be a delight?"

Amalia sighed. "Onkel Andreas told me about his love, Regina. We can't let Vater tear us apart the way they were."

Peter stroked her arm. "Once I make my fortune, he'll have no choice but to accept our marriage."

A sudden crash outside the window startled Amalia. She sat up straight, heart pounding. Peter stroked her arm again, trying to soothe her, but it took a moment before she regained her calm.

"I know many people dislike the wind," he said gently. "But why are you so afraid of it?"

She turned her head away, as if the answer brought shame.

Peter watched her, puzzled. What could his good, beautiful Amalia be hiding?

"Did something happen—when you were small?"

She shrugged, her voice barely above a whisper. "There are many reasons to fear the winds, Peter. They bring chaos wherever they go. Houses catch fire, crops fail, people lose their minds... and I get sick."

Peter didn't press her. She was private, and he respected that. Her thoughts and fears were hers to share in time. Instead, he pulled her close, wrapping his arms around her, wishing to shield her from whatever it was.

He whispered into her ear, "I'll do everything in my power to keep you safe."

Amalia turned back toward him and rested her head on his chest. The steady rhythm of his heartbeat calmed her racing thoughts. She wished they could stay like this forever—sheltered from the world and all its storms.

"It happened when I was eight," she began softly. "Ursula, my cousin Barbara, and I had played in the snow all day. That night, we slept in front of the fire at Barbara's house. I hung my mittens near the hearth and never thought twice about it."

She paused, her voice tightening with the weight of the memory.

"Then the foehn wind came while we were sleeping. I think the dry air made the mittens catch fire. When I woke, flames were everywhere. I screamed. Ursula was the only one who got out with me."

She felt Peter's arms tighten around her, drawing her closer.

"Once we were outside, I realized Barbara wasn't with us. I tried to run back in—to get her—but Herr Kubli held me down."

Peter didn't say anything—he just listened. And somehow, that was all she needed. After years of silence and shame, of burying the memory of Barbara and what had happened that night, something inside her finally felt free. The weight she'd carried for so long released into the firelit room and evaporated.

As if to honor the trust she'd given him, Peter began to kiss her like never before, and she willingly returned his affection.

In the next room, the old man lay snoring, lost in dreams of the past, while the young lovers explored each other and dreamed of all that was yet to come. They spoke of orchards and vineyards, of babies and open fields—everything that whispered of new life and bright horizons. A couple of times in the night, they woke to place wood on the fire—and each time, they added more to their dreams before drifting back into each other's arms.

Outside, the storm shrieked around the walls, threatening to undo the rocks on the roof and tell the world that they were defying Herr Grob's plans for his daughter's life. It toppled trees and did its best to blow away the Alpenhaus that had borne its fury for generations. But Amalia felt no fears as she snuggled deeper into Peter's chest. The fire warmed her back, while his tender care warmed her heart.

She knew this was where she belonged—in Peter Britt's arms, facing the storms of life together.

28 Rag Doll

The storm had come and gone, as swiftly as a dream. And like a dream, the time she'd shared with Peter felt far too short—fleeting, yet unforgettable. Something inside her had changed. She felt stronger now, braver, as though their time together had rekindled a flame she could carry forward into whatever came next.

By the time Dora returned up the mountain, the thin layer of snow had already blown away, leaving behind only damp earth and scattered branches. She said nothing about her son being alone with Amalia—if she felt concerned, she gave no sign. Unlike Herr Grob, Peter's family seemed to welcome their future union.

For the first time in a long while, Amalia felt what it was like to belong—not just to Peter, but to a family who accepted her with open hearts.

It was hard to part again, but this time they had a plan to stay in touch. Sending mail through Dora might raise suspicion, so they agreed that Amalia would communicate through Ursula instead. Letters would be sent and received under Ursula's name at the postmaster's house, then quietly passed on to Amalia. It was the safest way to keep their correspondence hidden from Herr Grob.

With Jakob waiting in the village, Peter had to leave almost as soon as his mother arrived. Dora disappeared inside to tend to Onkel Andreas, giving the lovers a few final moments alone. After one last embrace and whispered promises to write, Peter picked up his satchel and headed down the trail. Amalia stood on the porch, watching him go. Just as he reached the bend, he turned and gave her one final wave. She raised her hand to her lips and blew him a kiss, then stepped back inside the cabin—her heart full, yet already aching.

Unlike the night of the blood moon—when she'd been torn from his side and forbidden to speak to him again—this goodbye brought Amalia a quiet sense of relief. It wasn't final. Decisions had been made, promises exchanged, and plans laid to meet again. This time, there was hope. This time, it was only a matter of time.

Throughout the next month, Dora came and went, doing her best to care for those suffering from typhoid. No one understood the true cause of the illness. Many believed it came from bad air or spoiled food. Dora, however, was convinced that cleanliness made a difference. In her experience, households that kept things tidy seemed to suffer less, so she urged everyone to clean their homes thoroughly. Sometimes it helped; other times, it seemed to make no difference at all.

Amalia felt a wave of relief each time Dora returned safely. In a winter when typhoid spread like wildfire, it was no small miracle that she managed to stay well.

The false spring had vanished, just as the old man had warned. Each day, Amalia looked out, hoping for sunshine and blue skies, only to find white and gray as fresh snow quietly buried the memory of the once-warm, thawing earth.

On such days, it was hard to believe the sun had ever shone—that the storm had come and gone, and with it, Peter at his best: listening, serving, and offering her his l ove.

As she cared for Onkel Andreas, Amalia moved with even greater gentleness and kindness. Her renewed understanding of the old cattleman's heartbreak had forged a bond between them. Where she had once seen only a delirious old man, she now recognized a tender, childlike soul. She humored his songs and stories—and even shared a few of her own. Caring for him no longer felt like a chore, but an honor.

Amalia found herself in a season of waiting. Waiting for Dora to return from the village. Waiting for mail from Peter—delivered, for now, through his mother as long as she remained at the Alpenhaus. Waiting for Andreas to die. Waiting for spring.

She knew that when spring came, she would be expected to return to her father's household, just in case Peter should return. The thought that she'd had Peter all to herself, hidden from Herr Grob's knowledge, never failed to bring a smile to her face.

The rag doll had long been restored to its former glory and now sat peacefully in the rocking chair by the fire, a small symbol of transformation in a world still waiting to thaw.

During those quiet days of waiting, Amalia worked on the embroidery pattern her mother had given her at Christmas. With each careful stitch, she dreamed of the day she would hang it on the wall of the home she shared with Peter.

One morning, Amalia and Dora were startled by a knock at the door. Family members rarely knocked—they simply came in—and they had few visitors, unless someone had hiked over the mountain in need of warmth or refreshment. Dora had just stepped out of Andreas's room and gave Amalia a nod to answer it.

When she opened the door and saw Ursula standing there, Amalia froze. For a moment, words escaped her. She hadn't spoken to her friend since the night of the blood moon.

"It's Rosa!" Ursula paused to catch her breath after hurrying up the mountain. "The children have all been sick with fevers and coughs, but Rosa isn't getting better. She's asked for you."

Amalia's heart twisted at the memory of sweet-faced Rosa offering her the rose-colored quartz she still carried in her bag. She remembered the child's desperate, pleading eyes—and the wave of relief when she'd finally been able to breathe again.

Her thoughts turned to the missing herbs from her rucksack. She looked at Dora. "Do you have any hyssop and thyme?"

Dora nodded and quickly went to gather them, tying each bundle into a swath of linen.

"Go," she said softly, pressing the herbs into Amalia's hands. "May this child revive once again."

Amalia gathered her rucksack and embroidery, then, on impulse, rushed to the rocking chair where the rag doll sat. Tucking it into her bag, she hoped it might bring comfort—and maybe even a smile—to the little girl now fighting for her life.

The trek down the icy mountain, across the valley, and into the foothills took the better part of the morning. Amalia could only hope the child would still be alive when they arrived.

She and Ursula moved quickly—down one mountain and across to the next—saying little as they went. There was no time to speak of the past, not with a child's life hanging in the balance. Few words passed between them, but many prayers ascended.

Once again, an older sister opened the door and led them to the small figure lying on the cot in front of the fire. Just as before, little Rosa was struggling to breathe—but this time, her eyes lit up at the sight of Amalia.

This time, Ursula didn't need instructions. She set about heating water and preparing cough syrup with the herbs, while Amalia held a bowl of steaming water near Rosa's face to ease the child's breathing. The two friends moved in sync, working like a team. Words weren't necessary—they both knew what was required.

Just as before, it took time—time for the steam to loosen the congestion in Rosa's lungs before Amalia could offer her the syrup. This time, she crushed peppermint between her fingers and dropped it into the steaming water, releasing its sharp, soothing fragrance. Dora had recommended it before she left, and it seemed to be helping.

As the day wore on, Rosa began to breathe more easily. Before leaving, Amalia made sure her mother had plenty of syrup and a small bundle of dried peppermint, in case the treatment needed repeating.

Then, as she was saying goodbye, Amalia reached into her rucksack and pulled out the rag doll. She handed it to Rosa, who greeted the gift with a bright smile—even as a flicker of pain crossed Ursula's face.

As they walked back toward the village, Amalia sensed that Ursula had something on her mind. She braced herself to listen.

"How could you give that doll away?" Ursula's voice trembled—not with anger, but something deeper. "It's the only thing you have that's like the one Barbara had. Why can't you honor her memory? What's wrong with you? It's been twelve years since the fire, and you still won't talk about it."

Amalia doubted anything she said would satisfy Ursula. How could she explain the guilt she carried for leaving her mittens hanging too close to the fire? How could she admit that, in the darkest corner of her heart, she believed it was her fault Barbara hadn't awakened and escaped the flames like they had? Her shame had always felt too heavy, too dark to speak aloud. For years, she'd feared that if anyone knew the truth, they wouldn't love her. But now that she'd told Peter, something had changed. The secret no longer held her captive. She took a deep breath, searching for the words.

"What makes you think I don't care about Barbara? She was my cousin. I remember her every time I sense a foehn wind and recall how dry the air was. I think of her whenever I see Herr Kubli's pear orchard turning brown in autumn—because the leaves on those trees turned instantly when the hot wind blew through that day."

She swallowed hard, the words catching in her throat, tears filling her eyes.

"And for twelve years, I've seen that doll sitting in the corner of my room as a reminder. I've always wondered what I could've done—how I might have prevented her death. So please, don't tell me what I feel. And don't ever assume that I don't care."

They walked on in silence until Ursula finally said, "I'm sorry. I missed her so much—and I missed you too. You lived, but after the fire, you stopped spending time with me. It felt like I lost both of you."

Amalia had been so wrapped in her own shame and sorrow that she'd never considered how deeply Ursula might be hurting too. She stopped walking and reached for her friend. They embraced, tears rising in both their eyes—mourning what had been lost, and beginning to mend what remained.

Ursula continued to weep. "I'm sorry, Amalia. I never meant to turn you in on the night of the blood moon. I didn't know it was you."

Amalia paused and gave a faint smile. "Think of all the things that have come between us—famines, foehn winds, and death. If our friendship can survive all that, maybe we're meant to stay friends."

Ursula's tone suddenly brightened. "I have a secret, and I'm just dying to tell someone."

Amalia smiled, eager to share secrets of her own—but a flicker of curiosity passed through her. Was Ursula about to announce an engagement?

"You know how I've been working for Father Huber?" Ursula's eyes sparkled. "He's been paying me a small stipend, and I've been saving every bit of it. By next spring, the twins should be old enough to help with the younger kids—and I'm finally going to America."

Amalia was stunned. She'd heard Ursula talk about emigrating before, but she'd always assumed it was just girlish dreaming. Now it was clear—Ursula was serious. She wasn't waiting for permission from any man to decide how she would live her life.

Amalia couldn't help but admire her.

In response, Amalia shared her own secrets—of her wonderful time with Peter and their plans to marry in America. She asked Ursula to help her send and receive mail, and Ursula readily agreed.

They made a pact to hold each other's secrets and support one another in reaching their goals, whatever it took.

Amalia returned to the Alpenhaus with her heart full of joy—and her happiness only deepened when Dora handed her a letter. It was from Peter—a love letter, sealed and waiting in her hand, full of promise.

29 Darkness

It warmed Amalia's heart to hear from Peter again on a weekly basis. Postage wasn't cheap, so the most economical way to send a letter was a single folded sheet, sealed at the back with wax. Peter wrote his notes to Amalia at the bottom of his father's letters to his mother—and Amalia did the same beneath his mother's replies. It was a clever way to keep their correspondence hidden, in case the postmaster's wife might grow curious and tried to warm the seal to pry it open if she saw the young people's names. The elder Britts didn't seem to mind sharing their space on the page, and the young couple was grateful to exchange news—however brief, and despite the lack of privacy.

The winter had been long that year, but by early May, it seemed the sun was trying to make up for lost time. Within a week or two, the meadows turned green, and wildflowers began popping up everywhere.

One morning, Amalia sat outside with her tea, soaking in the warmth, when she heard the familiar sound of cowbells echoing up the mountain. Neighboring farmers were leading their herds to graze in the higher meadows.

Since Onkel Andreas had fallen ill, and because the family was preparing to emigrate, Kaspar sold off most of the Britt cattle, keeping only a couple of milk cows. The alpine pastures, however, were still valuable, and several neighboring farmers were eager to rent the grazing land for the season. The extra income eased the family's burden and allowed Kaspar to set aside more funds for the journey—while also relieving him of one more responsibility as he prepared for their departure.

Dora was usually out foraging by this time of year, but she hadn't gathered as many spring herbs as in the past—partly because she was busy caring for Andreas, and partly because they still had a good stock of dried herbs in the cellar.

Amalia welcomed the blue skies and the fresh green across the fields, but her heart felt heavy. The thought of returning to her father's house filled her with dread. She hated the obligatory dinners with Karl or other suitors. More than anything, she hoped she could keep her romance with Peter a secret—with Ursula's help.

Just as Amalia had suspected, it was only a matter of time before Dora returned with a note from her father, summoning her home. She knew he was worried about Peter coming back and didn't want them to see each other. A flicker of guilt passed through her, but it was quickly overtaken by the joy she felt every time she thought of that stormy night. It had only been two months, yet it already felt like a lifetime ago. Amalia hoped Peter would come home soon, but finding a way to see him again would be no easy task under Herr Grob's watchful eye.

She had only been home a day when Ursula came to visit. They slipped up to Amalia's room to whisper about their writing plans. While her friend was there, Amalia decided to compose a letter to let Peter know she was back home. Before leaving, Ursula promised to seal it and post it for her. If the postmaster's wife happened to get nosy, she might assume Peter and Ursula were exchanging letters now—which made for a convincing cover. Both girls agreed it was the safest way to keep Amalia's secret.

Within a week, Ursula returned with a letter tucked safely in her bag. She slipped it to Amalia upstairs, away from prying eyes. The girls agreed it would be safer for Amalia to start picking up her mail at Father Huber's, where there was no risk of Herr Grob witnessing an exchange.

As soon as Ursula left, Amalia unfolded Peter's letter and read it slowly, savoring every word. Then overcome with how much she missed him, she wept. After pressing a kiss to the page, she tucked it into the secret box beneath her bed.

Herr Grob had never approved of Amalia's charity work, and he liked it even less now that he expected her to prepare for marriage. Amalia knew he'd be furious if he caught wind of her ruse. To stay safe, she waited until her father left for work before making her way across the village to Father Huber's. She made it a point to be home in time for the evening meal—unless, of course, she was helping someone who was ill.

In the beginning, the plan worked perfectly—until Peter wrote that he might be heading home soon. Onkel Andreas had taken a turn for the worse and was not expected to live much longer.

And then, the letters stopped.

Amalia sent a few more, hoping he might still receive them. When no reply came, she wrote again—this time to his mother. Days passed, then weeks, with no word. She expected to find a note tucked into the fence any day. Each morning, after Herr Grob left for work, she slipped outside, lifted the rock, and checked the secret hiding place.

Day after day. Week after week. Nothing.

No word from Ursula. No note in the fence.

Amalia was confused, and yet she had no way to contact the Britts directly. Her father would grow suspicious if she even asked after Onkel Andreas. Ursula was concerned too. She promised to make a few inquiries—casually, so as not to raise suspicion—about the old man's health.

But as the silence stretched on, fear began to settle in Amalia's bones. It wasn't like Peter to stop writing. Something must have happened. Perhaps he was ill. Perhaps he'd fallen in some accident while crossing the Alps. With no letters sent to Ursula and no messages left in the fence, her imagination grew darker with each passing day.

At night, her thoughts raced. In the morning, she woke exhausted and nauseous from worry and dread. She felt certain that any day now, someone would bring news she never wanted to hear.

That day finally came.

When Amalia heard that Andreas Britt had passed away—and that the funeral had already taken place, her worry gave way to grief, and then to anger. Peter had been in town—and hadn't even tried to contact her.

She was overcome with confusion. Why hadn't he written? Why hadn't he come?

Had he found someone else?

Had her father threatened him?

Or—had he simply stopped wanting her, now that they had shared the most intimate of affections?

Even the Britt family kept their distance—whether out of grief for Onkel Andreas or in deference to Herr Grob's wishes, she couldn't be sure. Either way, the silence was unbearable. It felt strange that the family she had once belonged to had become so quiet.

But the worst part of her pain was having to keep up appearances with her own family—and with Karl. At every meal, every Sunday dinner, she had to paste on a cheerful smile, as if her heart weren't breaking.

At night, she stifled her sobs into her pillow, but even that brought no relief. Each morning, she woke to her grief all over again. And on some mornings, the ache in her stomach was so strong she had to slip out to the outhouse and quietly lose her breakfast, doing her best to make sure no one heard.

And then, one morning, it hit her.

It wasn't just the grief. It wasn't just the silence.

She was with child.

With child—and without a husband. A child Peter had once longed for, before he stopped writing to its mother.

Terror washed over her—not just because of what was happening to her body, but because of what might happen if anyone found out. No one would respect her. No one would believe she was a good Christian girl now. And her parents—especially her father—would be ashamed of her.

And what about Peter? Nausea washed over her as she remembered his eyes. The set of his firm jaw. The sound of his whisper in her ear that made her stomach flutter with exhilaration to be in his presence.

And now? Silence.

In the silence, she kept imagining—but what good were past memories with no hope for the future?

Not even Ursula could be trusted with this truth. The moment she told someone, the secret would no longer be hers.

One morning, she decided to check the fence again. Her fingers found nothing, but she willed them to keep searching, reaching farther through to the other side.

All she found was air.

She looked up at the blue sky—once her joy, and felt there wasn't enough sunshine to lighten the darkness washing over her.

A wave of grief crashed over her. She clung to the fence and began to weep.

Just then, the widow Brunner happened to pass by and paused at the sight of her.

"Are you ill, child?"

Amalia shook her head. She had no words to describe her loss, no way to explain the weight in her chest or the silence that surrounded her.

And there was no one she could tell.

Her heartache was hers alone.

30 Precipice

Despite getting no answer from Peter, Amalia continued to send letters through Ursula. They tried more than one address in France, but he never replied.

In the meantime, Amalia did her best to hide her expanding belly—but she knew it wouldn't be possible much longer.

Even Ursula hadn't noticed, which surprised Amalia. But then, they barely crossed paths. Between her duties for Father Huber and caring for her siblings, Ursula stayed busy. They exchanged letters and updates quickly, then went their separate ways. She had no time—or reason—to study her friend's waistline.

It was July when Ursula brought the news that the Britt family was selling off the furniture and cheesemaking supplies at the Alpenhaus. Amalia knew they must be planning to go to America for sure. She also knew how much the place meant to them, and the decision couldn't have been easy.

The Alpenhaus had served the Britt family for generations, though they had never owned it outright. Like many mountain huts in the canton, it was held under communal rights. It had to be passed on to another farming family who could tend the cows and put the land to good use.

Andreas Britt, and his fathers before him for generations, had managed the land. But now that Andreas was gone, it only made sense to hand the rights to someone else.

From the moment she realized she was with child, Amalia had one thought on her mind, and that was to tell Peter.

She was deeply disappointed that he had come back to the canton to help bury his uncle without seeing her. That hurt more than all the missing letters combined.

Part of her wanted to wait for just one more day, hoping he would show up and clear his good name, but she couldn't. Since he hadn't come looking for her, she would have to go looking for him.

If the Britt family was selling off the Alpenhaus supplies, perhaps someone there could tell her where he was—or whether he was even still around.

And if she couldn't find Peter, then she must find Dora.

If there was anyone she could trust and confide in besides Peter, it was Dora.

She waited until Herr Grob went to work and her mother had gone to visit a friend before making the trek up to the Alpenhaus.

It was a warm summer day, but as she climbed higher, the air grew cooler. The trail was full of memories—and all of them were good. That made Peter's silence even harder to bear.

Had he not enjoyed their talks and walks? How could he simply stop writing? It made no sense unless he'd found someone else.

Maybe her joke about the Fräulein in France wasn't so far from the truth.

The more she thought about it, the worse she felt.

Why did women have no rights? Why was it a woman's lot in life to carry the child—both in her body and in her heart—while men were free to move on?

Surely God was a man. He'd given little thought to what a woman must endure.

As she stepped into the clearing around the Alpenhaus, Amalia wasn't surprised to see cows grazing in the clover. That's how it had always been for generations.

What caught her off guard was the empty cabin.

There was no one in sight, and it was clear that the Britt family's belongings had been moved or sold. The door opened easily, but inside, the room stood hollow and bare.

Amalia wished she hadn't looked.

She would rather remember it as it had been—warm, lived-in, filled with the scent of cheese and woodsmoke and laughter. The way it felt when Andreas Britt still called it home.

Amalia's footsteps felt heavier with every step as she started back down the mountain. It seemed as though grief had taken root in her chest, and drained her of all possibilities.

On the way up, she'd felt a sense of hope—that no matter why Peter hadn't written, she might still find answers. But now, even that hope was gone. For all she knew, the entire family was already on their way to America.

Feeling sick to her stomach with grief, she stopped and looked out over the valley, as if she might catch a glimpse of Peter from the top of the precipice.

But all she could see was the church and the Walensee.

From her perch, she couldn't even tell if there were any boats on the lake—but in her mind, she saw Peter and his family stepping onto one, their backs turned, leaving the canton behind.

Leaving her behind.

The thought of him leaving her was more than she could bear. Her legs gave way beneath her, and she sank to the ground, tears streaming down her cheeks.

She hadn't been there long when a terrible idea came to her.

If she slipped and fell from the cliff, no one would ever know about the baby. It would end her life—but it would preserve her family's reputation. And she would never have to see the disappointment in Herr Grob's eyes again.

Her parents would grieve of course, but they wouldn't have to bear her shame.

Maybe it was the heat. Perhaps it was the emptiness of the Alpenhaus. But it was mostly the heartache of being left behind and forgotten that led her to such a thought. In her hot, thirsty, and delirious state, it felt like death was the only answer.

She'd die for the sake of her family.

Her death would save her reputation. And it would spare her parents the disgrace her life now carried.

She got up and stepped closer to the edge of the cliff.

It made her nervous to look down.

Before she took that final step, she decided to speak to Peter one more time—even if he couldn't hear her.

She opened the locket to take one last look at his face.

"Oh Peter, where are you? What have we done?"

Just as she braced herself to move forward, something fluttered deep within her.

She froze.

It was faint—like the brush of wings—but unmistakably real. Her hand flew to her belly as she realized what it was.

The baby was moving.

Her breath caught in her throat. For a moment, the world stood still.

Then, like a whisper on the wind, Rosa's voice echoed in her memory:

"Don't you wish you had a little child like me?"

A sob escaped her lips.

"Yes," she whispered. "Yes, I do want a little child like you."

She slowly stepped back from the cliff, trembling—shocked by what she had nearly done.

This child was hers and Peter's, created in love, on one of the most beautiful nights of her life.

Suddenly, she no longer cared what anyone thought.

If Ursula could go to America alone, then perhaps she could find her own way—or even strike a deal with Karl to protect her name and give the baby a home.

All her life, she'd tried to fit work around her father's rules. His rules and judgment had only given her pain. If he hadn't been so controlling, she would be a married woman and this child would be welcomed—by grandparents and a father.

Even if she could no longer count on Peter, she could count on herself.

She would begin by telling Herr Grob the truth.

No more sneaking. No more shame. No more obeying for the sake of her father's comfort.

From this moment on, she would live life on her terms with nothing to hide.

31 Sunday

AMALIA SENT A LETTER to Karl through Ursula, asking him to meet her near the church. It was a quiet spot on most days—save for Sundays—when the square filled with parishioners and chatter.

When Karl arrived, he seemed composed, if a little puzzled. Amalia took a breath and spoke with as much grace as she could muster.

"I must be honest with you, Karl. I have loved Peter for many years. I only agreed to consider your courtship because my father insisted. He believes I might grow to care for you in time—and perhaps I might. You have been nothing but kind. Of all the suitors he has approved, you are by far the most agreeable.

"But I would be wrong to give you false hopes. My heart belongs to another."

Karl's brow furrowed, but his voice remained gentle. "You surely didn't summon me here just to say that. What is it you truly wish to tell me?"

Amalia lowered her gaze. This was harder than she'd imagined. But for the sake of her child, she had to humble herself and find some means of protection—not only from the whispers of the townsfolk, but from Herr Grob himself.

There was no way to say it gently, so she blurted it out. "I am with child. And I have been abandoned by the father."

Karl nodded slowly. "So, you would become my wife, in exchange for me raising your child?"

Amalia's face flushed crimson. "Yes," she whispered.

He was silent for a moment while Amalia held her breath. She couldn't tell if he was angry, offended, or merely absorbing what she said.

At last, he spoke gently. "Do you remember when I told you I might emigrate to America one day? I wanted you to know that before we ever considered marriage. I believe you're offering me the same honesty now."

Relief flooded her mind. He wasn't offended. She had feared rejection—or even worse, scorn—but he seemed to understand.

She was about to ask if they could marry soon, given her condition, when he added, "If you're willing to go to America, I'm willing to raise your child as my own—and any others that may come to us. I'll do my best to care for you."

Amalia's heart sank.

Not only would she be agreeing to the voyage and all its unknowns, but she would be binding herself to a man for whom she felt no affection. And though he was kind, she could not imagine giving herself to him in the way a wife must.

"I don't want to cross the ocean with a baby," she said gently. "Could we wait until the child is old enough to stay near me and understand the dangers? I worry that a little one might wander too close to the rails—or fall ill at sea."

She didn't say it aloud, but in her heart, she hoped that waiting might buy her time—to think and pray, and maybe even change her fate.

Karl considered her words, then gave a slow nod. "I understand your concern, and I'll honor that—so long as my circumstances allow it. But if my debts begin to outweigh my earnings, we may have no choice but to leave, as so many others have."

Amalia had little choice but to agree. What mattered now was securing the marriage, so she could face the coming winter—she now had a child to protect.

They set the wedding for August, only a few weeks away. Karl promised to join her for the Sunday meal, where they would make their engagement known to her family.

As Amalia walked home, a strange sense of relief settled over her. Yet questions still crowded her mind. Where would they live? Did Karl have a home of his own, or would she be expected to share a roof with his mother?

Though her feet still traveled the familiar paths of Glarus, her world no longer felt the same. It was as if she had crossed into a foreign country—uncharted, uncertain, and entirely of her own making—with no sign of Peter on the horizon.

Sunday came, and Amalia was so nervous she could scarcely lift a hand in the kitchen. Her mother, unaware of the storm brewing beneath the surface, took up the tasks with cheerful ease—kneading dough for birnbrot and humming a hymn, as though all were well with her daughter.

Karl had agreed to let Amalia take the lead in speaking to Herr Grob. They both expected he would be pleased by their engagement—but once he learned she was with child, his delight would surely turn to fury.

The conversation drifted from the weather, to the rising price of coffee, to the growing number of emigrants leaving for America.

"I've no use for those who abandon our beautiful Glarus," Herr Grob said, his tone sharp. "I suspect those Glarners who go will come to regret it."

He cast a pointed glance at Amalia, making it plain the remark was meant for her—and for Peter. Rumors about the Britt family's plans to emigrate were spreading quickly through the village.

Maria Grob rose to clear the dinner plates and stepped into the kitchen to fetch the birnbrot, while Amalia quietly set out the cheese and poured the coffee.

But Herr Grob wasn't finished. As though she hadn't heard him the first time, he added with a sneer, "I do hope, my dear mousekin, that you'll find a more suitable husband than that wandering artist."

Amalia froze. Her cheeks burned. She could take no more.

"Vater—stop it!" she cried. "I love Peter—and I'm carrying his child!"

From the kitchen came a loud crash as Maria dropped the birnbrot and the plate shattered on the stone floor.

Herr Grob stood abruptly, his chair scraping harshly behind him.

"What did you say?" His voice was loud and it sliced through the room like a knife. "You've disgraced yourself—and this family—with such shameless conduct!"

Amalia flinched, but willed herself not to look away.

Maria remained frozen in the doorway, her hands trembling, crumbs of birnbrot still clinging to the broken plate at her feet.

Herr Grob turned to Karl. "I owe you an apology. My daughter is not worthy of you."

Karl rose slowly, his face pale. "Sir, I am offering her protection—to do what another man did not. To give her the honor she deserves."

Herr Grob turned back to Amalia. The red in his face began to fade.

"Then go ahead. Marry him. The sooner the better. And may heaven have mercy on your soul."

32 The Letter

On her wedding day, Amalia finally received her mother's family Bible as part of her trousseau. She had immediately tucked the dried starflower between its pages—for good luck and to honor her fragile dreams for what might have been. She looked forward to recording the birth of her firstborn child in its pages.

Kaspar Britt was born on December 7, 1843. Karl wasn't in the room—only her mother, Ursula, and the midwife stood by her side.

As soon as the baby was placed in her arms, Amalia kissed his damp forehead and counted every tiny finger and toe. Then she whispered with a trembling smile,

"You were born almost exactly nine months after your father's birthday."

She named him Kaspar, after Karl's given name. He would wear their family name of Grob, and no one would suspect he was Peter's child. Yet hidden from public view, and soon to be quietly inscribed in the church archives, his name was entered as Kaspar Britt.

The newlyweds had set up house in Karl's family home, and to Amalia's relief, he had asked his mother to move in with his sister—giving them space to adjust to the many changes in their lives.

Baby Kaspar was Amalia's greatest joy. Each day, he grew stronger and more like Peter. It was impossible not to think of his father when she looked into his eyes. The resemblance was undeniable. And with that resemblance came a quiet ache. She couldn't help but wonder if Karl would ever truly love Kaspar as his own—or if anyone could love him the way his real father would have.

Each day, Karl went to work, came home, ate supper, and went to bed. He rarely spent any time with her except to meet his needs.

Amalia sat brushing out her long hair one evening. Karl had suggested they go to bed early, and she suspected it wasn't only for sleep. She smoothed her hair, slipped into her nightdress, and unfastened the locket from around her neck. As her fingers traced the delicate chain, she thought of Peter's proposal.

The necklace was easy to conceal beneath her bodice, and few had ever seen it. It struck her as strange that Karl had never asked about it. He never inquired as to what it was, nor whose likeness it held. And she had never offered to tell him.

Perhaps he never asked because he had secrets of his own. She glanced toward the bed and saw that Karl had already fallen asleep, his mouth open in a snore. In that moment, she realized this man had no secrets. There was no mystery about him. He was as predictable as the stone wall around her father's house: strong, consistent, and un-wavering. Why couldn't she feel content with such a man?

As Amalia slid into bed beside him, she felt no desire to warm her feet against his back or curl into his embrace. She pulled the duvet over her shoulder and lay still, marveling at how she slept just as she had when she was a girl—alone, self-contained, untouched. The only difference now was the loudly snoring man on the other side of the bed.

When she finally drifted off to sleep, Amalia dreamed of Peter. They were living in America. Their home was sur-rounded by fruit trees and a sprawling vineyard. Sunlight bathed the fields, while the laughter of children echoed around them and a baby played at their feet.It was such a beautiful dream. She felt so full of peace and joy, until the cries of her baby jolted her awake.

Quickly, she jumped up and scooped baby Kaspar into her arms, hoping to soothe him before he woke Karl. As she rocked him in the dark of the night, her own tears mingled with his. And yet, even in that moment, she had no regrets. If she had the chance all over again, to meet Peter Britt down by the Walensee, knowing everything she knew now, she would do it all over again—for love.

When Kaspar was just six months old, a letter arrived from a Grob cousin in America. Because of the high cost of postage, such letters were rare, and typically addressed to the entire family in one message. Word spread quickly, and before long, the entire Grob clan gathered to hear it read aloud.

Hurry, Amalia! We don't want to miss anything!

Karl's impatience irritated her. If he was in such a hurry, why didn't he help by carrying the baby? She quickly wrapped Kaspar in an extra blanket and trailed behind him.

Though it was early summer, the Alpine breeze still carried a chill. All the Grobs in the canton were gathering at her father's house to hear the letter read aloud.

Many crowded the doorway because there was only standing room for everyone. Amalia was surprised her father had even agreed to host the gathering, given how deeply he despised the idea of emigration. They were meeting there because her father, still the family patriarch, was too weak to travel and worn down by consumption.

Karl had insisted she hear the letter in person. Amalia agreed because she couldn't deny a sick man the chance to see his only grandson. She hoped now that she was married and settled, Herr Grob would no longer feel the need to control her. Despite all the excitement in the air, she had no plans for going to America.

The cousin with the letter climbed onto a chair so everyone packed into the crowded house could hear him. A hush fell over the room. All eyes turned toward him in anticipation, eager to hear a firsthand account of America from someone they actually knew.

He began to read, his voice steady:

The land stretches flat and broad—as far as the eye can see. Perfect for growing wheat, oats, barley, and every kind of vegetable. Even fruit trees thrive here. The seasons are mild and predictable. And best of all—no foehn winds to stir up sickness or trouble.

Amalia tried to still her wiggling son while the letter continued.

It described every kind of farming and weather imaginable in America.Once there, it seemed, one could choose to live in the snowy north—or in the warm south, where the summers stretched on and on all year.

The room full of Glarners gasped, wide-eyed at the possibilities.

When the cousin had finished reading, a long silence settled over the room.

The Grob men sat in quiet awe, dreaming of all that might be possible—if only they had flat land to farm. And the women, seated beside them, offered silent prayers to God that their husbands would not be tempted to pull up roots.

Karl was unusually quiet that night. Amalia feared he was thinking of moving to America. Now that she was settled in her own home, and raising a child, she didn't want to leave Switzerland. It had never been her dream to begin with.

As she was combing her hair and preparing for bed, Karl finally asked the question she'd been dreading.

"Amalia, what do you think about going to America?"

She took a deep breath and spoke firmly.

"I think if the sovereign God wanted us to be Americans, we would have been born there."

Karl turned to face her. "Surely you believe we have some choices in life."

"Yes," she said slowly, "we have choices over small things. But where we come from? That was never ours to choose."

"Oh, come on, if that were true, none of us would have ancestors from England or Germany."

He had a point, and she didn't wish to argue. Instead, she shifted to their agreement.

"I can't imagine taking a baby on a ship," she said softly. "Think how active he is—and how hard it would be to keep him from falling over the edge. We can't go until he's older."

She hoped that would hold him off. Perhaps by the time Kaspar was old enough to travel, Karl would have buried his wanderlust in his work and grown content with their life in Glarus. Wasn't that the very reason her father had urged her to marry Karl in the first place?

Karl continued to speak, as her fingers fell on the locket around her neck and her thoughts drifted to Peter.

She'd heard he hadn't left yet—that the Britts were still raising funds for the journey. It took a long time to get ready for such a move. There was also a rumor that Dora had fallen ill, which could delay their departure even longer.

She wondered if she dared to pay Dora a visit. Surely the older woman would already have tried any herbs that might help her. In any case, visiting the sick was considered a neighborly duty.

Suddenly, she realized Karl had grown quiet—and was looking at her with growing impatience.

Amalia tried to wear a calm facade as she listened to Karl's reasoning. Many of his arguments mirrored those she'd once heard from the Britt family.

"Do you not see why this matters?" he pressed. "The famines are getting worse. That means fewer buyers here, while in America, there's so much work—they never have enough hands."

"But we agreed," she said firmly. "You promised to wait until the child was old enough to stay away from the rails. He can't even walk yet—but it's only a matter of time."

She'd never seen Karl's face grow red like her father's.

As he stepped toward her, she flinched, fearing that he would strike her.

Instead, he grabbed the chain at her neck and tore it off, leaving a sharp burn where it scraped off her skin.

He opened the locket and stared at the tiny portrait of Maria Grob.

Amalia held her breath, hoping he wouldn't lift out that picture and discover the one of Peter.

"Did he paint this for you? Is that why it's so precious that you wear it day and night?"

Reeling from shock and pain, Amalia fought to hold back her tears.

Karl tossed the locket onto the bed and stormed out of the house, slamming the door behind him.

His shouting had awakened the baby.

As Kaspar's cries rose through the room, Amalia cradled him, her own tears falling freely.

With trembling hands, she picked up the locket and broken chain, tucking them into her secret box beneath the bed, wondering how to contain the fragments of all that had been broken.

33 Alpenrose

It was late July by the time Amalia gathered the courage to visit Dora. Carrying baby Kaspar on one arm, she juggled a basket on the other. The basket contained a jar of warm broth, wrapped in a towel, and made from Dora's own recipe. It was the concoction Dora prepared for those who refused to eat much. Amalia's heart beat with concern for the woman who'd been her friend for so many years. If only she could create the right potion and somehow extend the life of her mentor.

As she walked down the hill toward the Britt farm, she fought back emotions stirred by memories of visiting Peter in the past. She wondered where he was. Had he returned to check on his mother? Or was he still traveling? The thought of seeing him made her nervous. It was one reason she'd put off this visit for so long.

Even if she did see him, what could she possibly say or do that would change anything? Speaking to him alone would be inappropriate now that she was another man's wife. Married women with any sense of propriety didn't speak to men who were not their husbands.

As the mother of Peter's son, she longed to show him her pride and joy. She felt he deserved to know the truth, but there was little chance of telling him without creating a scandal. And now with Peter's mother ill, and her own father in poor health, she didn't wish to do anything that would embarrass either family.

As she continued down the old, rocky path to the Britt cottage, Amalia's thoughts drifted toward Karl and the night he had ripped off her locket. He'd returned later with an apology, but even now, neither of them had spoken about the locket's origin. She knew Karl's deepest frustration was his growing dream of moving to America—while she refused to leave until Kaspar was older, if even then. It had never been her dream to leave the canton. Her only motivation to go had been to marry Peter.

Amalia's reluctance left Karl in a quandary. He didn't want to force her, and he knew that preparing for such a monumental journey would be nearly impossible with a resistant wife. Within a few days, he had let the topic drop, but Amalia knew the matter wasn't settled.

Anna Britt met her at the door, speaking in hushed tones.

"Dora is quite frail now and confined to bed. The doctor says she isn't long for this world."

Amalia's heart sank. It was troubling to find the mistress of potions and herbal remedies unable to heal herself.

"Is her husband here?" She was careful not to mention Peter's name.

"No," Anna replied. "Kaspar wrote, but no one knows how long it will take them to return."

Amalia paused to steady herself and take a deep breath before entering the bedchamber.

Despite the pain in her eyes, Dora greeted Amalia with a cheery smile.

"Ah, there you are, daughter! I've missed you!"

Amalia's eyes blurred with tears at the affectionate term. She wasn't sure she deserved it, but she was relieved to see there were no hard feelings between them. She propped baby Kaspar on a chair, then reached out to Dora's offered hand.

"I brought you some of that healing broth you taught me to make. Would you like to try it?"

Dora gave a faint nod.

Amalia tapped the spoon against the side of the bowl and stirred in a pinch of wild marjoram—just like Dora had taught her.

"I'd feel better if I could mix the right potion for you."

"Ah, but perhaps the Divine, in His sovereignty, has another plan."

Amalia pressed her lips together to hold back her thoughts. Every time someone mentioned God's will, she spiraled into anger and despair.

If it was God's will for Dora to die, was her father's rejection of Peter also God's will? Was every illness, every cruel twist of fate, some part of the divine plan? Where did God's will begin, and where did it end? Did people not have any say in the shaping of their lives?

She held the spoon to Dora's dry, cracked lips while the worn woman took a small sip. Amalia reminded herself to apply lanolin before she left.

After a second sip, Dora turned away. No one else was in the room, yet she spoke in a whisper.

"You mustn't worry if I don't get well. I'm ready to rest. My husband wants to go to America, but I'm terrified of tossing about in a ship. Once I'm gone, his dream can come true. It's best for both of us this way."

Amalia felt a pang in her stomach to think that two people who had shared a lifetime together might soon be separated by an ocean in death.

She thought of Peter. The idea of being parted from him forever still made her stomach clench. She couldn't bear to think about it. But Dora looked so tired. If the idea of Jakob leaving gave her peace, Amalia couldn't bring herself to take that away.

Dora took another swallow of broth, then gently motioned for Amalia to take it away. She wiped Dora's mouth before smoothing a layer of balm over her lips.

"Your inability to heal me is not your fault. You are still a great healer, and I'm proud of you."

Amalia shook her head.

"I don't feel like much of a healer, Dora."

Dora gave her a weary smile.

"Ah, my dear, that is the brunt of this life—that healers cannot always heal themselves."

Then her eyes brightened.

"Can you bring your baby closer?"

When Amalia held little Kaspar up to his grandmother, she saw a flicker of recognition in Dora's eyes. Her tired face suddenly radiated with joy.

"So, he is who I thought he was! Thank you for bringing him to me!"

Dora reached out her hand, while the baby grasped her finger and smiled. Dora's eyes filled with tears.

"He looks exactly like his father did at that age."

Amalia saw an opportunity.

"Will you please tell Peter about his son?"

"Yes, of course, I will, dear!"

After a few minutes of sweet-talking the baby, Dora looked so spent that Amalia feared she might have over-stayed her welcome. She gathered her bowl and child, preparing to slip quietly out the door while the sick woman closed her eyes to rest.

Then Dora opened them once more to whisper.

"Remember to be like the Alpenrose. Stand strong throughout all the storms of your life."

Amalia went home with a sense of satisfaction that Peter would finally know about his child.

But it was not to be.

The next day, a message arrived from Anna, informing her that Dora had passed away in the night, before her husband and son could return home.

34 Treasure Box

The canton of Glarus buzzed with activity in the spring. A sense of urgency hung in the air. The winter had been harsh and bitter cold, with scarce food and widespread sickness. Many Glarners had not survived.

Driven by the twin fears of disease and starvation, the emigration pact gained momentum. Nearly every day, Amalia saw neighbors selling off their furniture and packing supplies for the journey. Most hung on to practical items like cookware and cheese-making tools, unsure of what they might need in the new land.

The Glarus Emigration Society sent leaders ahead to scout for land, but some colonists were not willing to wait. Hoping to plant crops and begin farming while it was still spring, a large group set sail while the scouts were still searching for ground to claim.

Other families, like the Britts, chose to go on their own, without any assistance from the Glarus Emigration Society.

They spent their life savings to buy passage to America, determined to start a new life and avoid another winter in Glarus.

In early April, the Britt family gathered the few belongings they had left and prepared to travel down the Linth Canal.

In the early morning light, Peter waited in line with his family. This was only the first step of a twenty-four-day journey to Le Havre, France, where they would eventually board a ship bound for America. But leaving the canton had not come without pain.

Jakob Britt paused and looked back at the Alps, drawing in a deep breath. His beloved Dora was buried beside Andreas behind the Alpenhaus. With both of them gone, there was nothing left to keep him from chasing his dream to see what America was like.

Jakob's eldest son, Kaspar, felt strangely empty-handed after selling all the cows and furniture. It was hard to believe everything they owned now fit into the leather bag tucked inside his pocket. On his back, he carried blanket rolls and a large rucksack filled with dried fruits and Schabziger cheese that Anna had packed for the journey. She figured if they had nothing else to eat with their potatoes, at least they could flavor it with their favorite cheese.

As Kaspar's wife, Anna, stepped onto the barge, she carried one screaming baby in her arms and clung tightly to another child's hand. Rolling her eyes to her husband, she signaled that she already felt exhausted. It had taken all her strength to prepare the food and ensure the children had enough warm clothing to survive a month at sea. Kaspar reached out to take the older child's hand, hoping to give his wife a reprieve.

Peter was the last to step onto the barge. He paused to study the Alps, bathed in the soft Alpenglow of early morning. He wanted to remember every detail, so that someday, he could pull out his sketches and paint them in all their glory.

As the last stars faded and sunlight crept higher over their peaks, each golden ray made his heart sink a little lower.

This wasn't how he'd planned it.

The bag he carried with all his worldly possessions felt heavier with each step. He would gladly give it all away—just to have Amalia beside him.

Until now, he'd always come home. He had always carried the quiet hope that, somehow, someday, he might catch Amalia alone and have one final conversation.

But now that she was a married woman with a child, there could never be a proper moment for them to speak—not in Glarus, not anywhere.

He already knew there was no future for him in the canton, but now he wondered if there was any place in the world for him without her.

By the time the call came to board, the sun had fully risen. Peter turned to take one last look at his homeland. The clear blue sky and the snow-capped peaks stood in their beauty as if daring him to stay. He noticed brown and white cows scattered among the rolling green hills, waiting to move up to higher ground.

He, too, was waiting to move on, to go farther than he'd ever gone before in his twenty-six years. He knew that if this quest failed, there would be nothing left to return to—the Alpenhaus was gone, and his boyhood home in the village had already been sold.

Obstalden—with its sweeping views of the Walensee and the sunlit Alps—would go on without him.

This leaving was unlike any he had known before. It left his heart hollow—echoing with what and whom he couldn't take with him.

When they got off the barge, the Britt family hired a wagon to carry their belongings across Switzerland and into France. The journey was slow and tiring—especially with Kaspar's wife, children, and a baby along. The baby cried almost constantly, and the older children were shy and overwhelmed by the unfamiliar sights and smells.

Peter did his best to play with them, keeping them distracted from the long, tedious days on the road.

At night, they slept outdoors beside the wagon, wrapped in their bedrolls beneath the stars. Before reaching the port, they made one last stop—to purchase a few more supplies, knowing that food would not be provided once they boarded the ship.

Back in Obstalden, Amalia took another sip of tea and slid a small package of herbs across the table to Ursula.

"I know it's only a matter of time before you leave," she said gently. "I wanted to give you some of the best remedies Dora taught me. I've included the recipes—so you can make your own in the new world."

Ursula set down her cup and blinked back tears. "I'm not ready to say goodbye yet. I'll be here for at least another month." She hesitated. "Did you hear? The Britt family left about a month ago."

Amalia nodded. "They should be boarding the ship any day now."

Her throat tightened at the thought of Peter leaving—perhaps forever.

Ursula, sensing the sorrow behind her friend's silence, reached across the table and took her hand.

"If I hear anything about him once I get to America," she said softly, "I'll write you and tell you everything I know."

She hadn't admitted it to anyone, but Amalia had been counting the days. She realized this might be the very day Peter set sail for America. Whatever remained unsaid between them now seemed destined to stay that way.

Even so, no matter how hard she tried, she couldn't get Peter out of her mind.

Then came a knock at her door.

It was Fridolin. Her little brother had grown into a handsome young man of fourteen. She greeted him with a smile—until she saw the expression on his face.

"What's wrong, brother?"

"It's Vater. The doctor told me to get you. He thinks it won't be long, and Vater wants to read his will to us."

Amalia pulled a warm sweater over Kaspar's head and grabbed his hand, pulling him all the way up the hill to her childhood home. When they reached the door, the doctor greeted her and informed her that her father was extremely weak.

Once again, Amalia gathered her composure before entering the bedchamber. She was weary of death and partings. First it was Onkel Andreas, then Dora, and now her father—must everyone she loved either die or leave?

She was unprepared to see Herr Grob so frail. He had always seemed larger than life. From her earliest memories, he had stood tall, willow stick in hand, asserting his will over her world.

Now, watching her father fade, she found herself wishing she could restore him to his former strength—because despite everything, he had sheltered her, provided for her, and in his own way, he had loved her.

Herr Grob called for Fridolin to get his treasure box from the study. Once it was in the room, it took several minutes to navigate the many locks. Fridolin seemed as new at this as Amalia—apparently, Herr Grob didn't trust anyone.

When the last lock was finally unlatched, Fridolin pulled out a stack of papers and letters.

Before the will could be read, Herr Grob coughed hard and long, and Amalia felt sick at the sight of the blood on the napkin her mother used to wipe his mouth.

When the sick man finally caught his breath, he motioned for Fridolin to come closer and sorted through a pile of papers. From within it, he drew a bundle of letters tied with a leather cord and gestured for Amalia to take them.

She stepped forward, puzzled, and looked down. The handwriting was unmistakably Peter's.

But what was her father doing with them?

Then she saw her own letters, addressed to Peter through Ursula—and her breath caught.

And in that instant, everything became clear.

Herr Grob had intercepted their letters. He had kept them—hidden them—all this time.

The room spun. Rage flooded her body as she struggled to steady herself. She once lied to her father about their secret engagement—but he had done something far worse. He'd stolen Peter's letters and tricked her into marrying Karl.

Amalia staggered under the weight of it. She had never received Peter's letters—and he had never received hers. She had believed he abandoned her. Yet all the while, he must have believed that she had betrayed him.

Her throat burned with acid. She thought she might be sick.

"Vater! How could you?"

"I'm sorry, Amalia. I know you don't understand, but from the day you were born, you were the apple of my eye. I couldn't bear the thought of you marrying that wandering artist and sailing off to America. We'd never see you again."

He paused, overcome by a fit of coughing. When he finally spoke again, his voice was barely more than a whisper.

"Ah, my Amalia... you must feel betrayed. But please know—I only did it to protect you. Just as you once lied and deceived me, I felt I had no choice but to deceive you. But you see, it all turned out well after all. You have a good husband who provides for you... and a beautiful son."

"But Vater—this is Peter's son. He had a right to know."

"Ah, Amalia... can't you see? I did it out of love. Only love."

Amalia wanted to scream—to ask if it was truly love for her, or for himself. But another violent cough overtook him, and when he pulled the kerchief from his mouth, it was soaked with blood and she ached to realize the doctor was right.

"Can you forgive me?" he rasped.

With tears stinging her eyes, Amalia lied to her father for the last time.

"Of course, Vater. I forgive you. Now lie back and rest."

Amalia clutched the letters in one hand, and her son with the other, as she marched out of the room. She passed her sobbing mother on the way to the door but didn't stop to embrace her.

There would be time for that later.

Whether her father had left her money or property, she didn't stay to find out. None of it mattered—not now. The only thing that mattered was the bundle of letters pressed tightly in her hand.

It didn't matter that her father was dying.

It didn't matter that she was married to someone else.

What mattered was the fact that Peter had not abandoned her.

He had never given up on her.

Those letters were a lifeline to a drowning woman.

As long as she knew Peter loved her, she could survive anything.

She carried a tired Kaspar home and put him down for a nap. Then she sat on the back stoop to read the letters.

The spring air carried a cool breeze up from the Walensee. She paused on the porch, noticing that her favorite yellow violets had begun to bloom.

She decided to read the last letter first—she wanted to know Peter's last thoughts before he stopped writing.

Her heart sank when she saw the date.

It was the week before her wedding.

My dearest and good Amalia,

How I long to see your face—not fixed in a painting, but close to mine, where I can study every flicker of light that lives in your eyes.

I am at a loss. I have not heard from you in months. Your father has forbidden all contact, and though I trusted Ursula would see my letters safely to you, I now wonder why none have been returned.

There never was—nor shall there ever be—a Fräulein in Paris. I may paint many faces, but none compare to yours. My heart holds no room for another. In my eyes, there is only—always—you.

Glarus has lost all joy without your presence. If I do not hear from you soon, I fear I shall have no choice but to go to America without you—though I would go with neither hope nor happiness.

Ever and only yours,

Peter

P.S. I shall never forget my birthday. That was the most wonderful night of my life. I live for the day I might hold you in my arms again.

Tears slipped down Amalia's cheeks as the truth took root.

Peter had never abandoned her.

He had planned for her.

He had loved her, all along.

Her heart stilled as something soft and white fell onto the page.

Looking up, she saw pear blossoms drifting through the air like snowflakes—just as they had the day Peter first walked her home from the Alpenhaus.

She drew a deep breath, drinking in the scent of spring.

It filled her with new life and the quiet hope of beginning again.

She rose to make Karl's favorite supper—and to tell him that she was finally ready to go to America.

35 Voyage

Le Havre, France, May 5, 1845

The name of the ship was *The Rose*. What might have seemed a fitting name for their journey felt painfully ironic to Peter.

Always a lover of nature, he admired roses—but he knew two women who loved flowers even more than he did, and neither of them was with him. He wondered how he would ever get one of them out of his mind—especially when every flower reminded him of her.

Once in line, Peter thought his eyes must be deceiving him. A few yards ahead, waiting to board the ship, a young woman was dressed much like the women of Obstalden—in practical dark clothing. Something about the way she moved, with her long skirts and braided hair, looked very familiar.

He was disappointed when she turned around. Not only was her face different, but she was speaking French.

Kaspar shook his head. "For a moment, I thought that was your Amalia."

Peter felt his face flush. "Well, she is no longer my Amalia—she's another man's wife."

He felt a mixture of anger and love for her, even though she was beyond his reach.

Later that afternoon, the young woman passed by them again with her sister and mother. She made eye contact with Peter, then lowered her head coyly in a subtle attempt at flirtation.

Kaspar nudged his brother. "Go talk to her."

But Peter shook his head. "There is no one for me but Amalia. I expect to live a very solitary life."

"Ah, come on," Kaspar insisted. "I know you loved her, but she's not the only woman in the world."

Peter's jaw grew tight. "Love her—not loved. And she's the only woman in the world as far as I'm concerned."

Kaspar laughed. "I guess we'll see. We're going to a new land with many new women to choose from. I'll keep a record of your words, little brother."

Later that night, in the hold of the ship, Peter tossed and turned on his bunk. His uneasiness had nothing to do with the ocean waves—for they'd barely left port, and the waters were still calm.

He had thought he'd be happy to be on his way to the land of opportunity, but his heart was heavy. How many times had he dreamed of this day?

Was it possible to be both excited and grief-stricken at the same time?

He had so many plans, but without Amalia, they seemed beyond his reach. Everything he had dreamed about and hoped for was connected to the two of them—building a home, starting a family, building a life together.

It was painful to realize the love of his life had slipped through his hands and had chosen to join her life with another.

The urge to punch a hole in one of the shipping barrels surrounding his bed surged within him.

The air in the cabin felt stuffy. He needed to find some air.

Sitting up and sorting through his satchel, he found what he was looking for among the drawings of the Alps and the people of Obstalden—he found the braided lock of Amalia's hair.

Holding it up to his nose, he breathed in her unique scent. It still smelled faintly of the natural oils she made from her favorite flowers.

Then he pulled on his boots and stumbled up to the deck.

The sea was calm at the moment, but there was no moon—neither red nor white. But the stars were out, and they reminded him of that night on the Walensee, where he first fell in love with a simple girl who laughed at his jokes.

What he wouldn't give to go back in time and try to make amends.

Of course, he wouldn't know where to begin. He was a Britt—the son of a farmer, who was the son of a farmer.

He couldn't think of anything he could've done to change Herr Grob's mind.

By emigrating to America, Peter, his father, and his brother were breaking a family tradition of farming in the Alps that had lasted for hundreds of years.

Peter noticed that he was still holding Amalia's hair in his hand, and his eyes grew misty as he realized he was separated from her now more than ever.

How he ached to take care of her, but he could think of no way to mend the distance between them. So he opened his hand, kissed her braid one last time, and tossed it into the sea.

They had been separated. First by her father. Then by marriage. And now—by an ocean.

If the Alps could speak,
they would tell tales of forbidden love,
torn apart by the will of others.

But if the moon could sing,
she would rise into a full yodel—
about sweet, tender kisses
and aching hearts of lovers,
forever intertwined
in each other's dreams.

Author's Note

ALTHOUGH PETER BRITT HAS been gone for over a hundred years, he remains larger than life in Southern Oregon. He left behind his good name, a thriving fruit and vineyard industry, a legacy through his children, and a rich collection of photographs that chronicle a way of life now nearly forgotten.

I have tried to stay true to what is known about Peter and Amalia. Stories in Southern Oregon describe Peter supporting the musical arts as well as the visual, so I worked his love of music into their story. Because Peter once painted Amalia as the Madonna—and because they exchanged letters, a locket, and a lock of her hair—I wove these tender real-life details into the novel.

Much less is known about Amalia Grob. Her mystery is what inspired The Alpenhaus. I imagined her life in Switzerland—young, in love, defying her father's wishes, and carrying the weight of her choices. When archaeologists uncovered a collection of apothecary bottles on the

Britt homestead, it sparked the idea that healing, nature, and resilience might have been part of her story as well.

To fill out their early love story, I have taken creative liberties. The most daring is the suggestion that Peter was the father of Amalia's first child. This choice is based on a Geneanet entry listing her firstborn son as Kaspar Britt, born December 7, 1843—exactly nine months after Peter's birthday on March 12 of that same year. Amalia's father refused to allow her to marry Peter and persuaded her to marry his cousin, Kaspar Grob (Karl, in this book), on August 22, 1843—four months before the child was born. Given the timing of these events, Peter's paternity seems a plausible possibility.

This book is only the beginning of their journey. I hope you'll enjoy the next installment, *Independence Days*, as Peter and Amalia cross oceans and face the choices that will shape their future.

May their lost dreams awaken something hopeful in you, too.

Acknowledgments

I'M INDEBTED TO ALL the storytellers and historians who have worked to preserve Peter Britt's legacy and, in turn, provided the foundation and inspiration for this novel.

These include, but are not limited to, the following resources:

Historic Jacksonville

https://www.historicjacksonville.org/

Southern Oregon Historical Society

https://sohs.org/

Patrick Wild at Glarus Family Tree

https://www.glarusfamilytree.com/

Carolyn Kingsnorth, "*Pioneer Profiles: Peter Britt*"

https://www.historicjacksonville.org/pioneer-profiles/

Book:

Alan Clark Miller, *Photographer of a Frontier: The Photographs of Peter Britt*. Eureka, CA: Interface California Corporation, 1976.

Also by Cherilyn Christen Clough

Chasing Eden: A Memoir

To UnEat an Elephant: A Memoir

Independence Days: Where Lost Dreams
Awaken 2

About the Author

CHERILYN CHRISTEN CLOUGH FELL in love with Historic Jacksonville while living in Southern Oregon for ten years. Walking on the same ground as Peter and Amalia once did, inspired her to imagine their love story. She now resides in Portland, Oregon, where she works with a somewhat sketchy assistant—Maggie, a Siberian cat, who has atrocious typing skills and frequently kicks the mouse to the floor so she can stretch across the desk.

www.ingramcontent.com/pod-product-compliance
Lightning Source LLC
Chambersburg PA
CBHW061755190726
48289CB00007B/1954